Other books by
Charles C. Fletcher:

Out West and Back

The Panther on Cold Mountain and Other Stories

Little Sam Mountain

Little Sam Mountain — The Journey

The Sheriff

Grassy Top Mountain

Little Sam Mountain — Living Their Dream

These books are available from Ingram, Amazon.com,
Baker & Taylor, Barnes & Noble, and directly from the author.

Charles C. Fletcher
2310 Harris Circle NW
Cleveland, TN 37311
423-476-6835
ccfletch9@yahoo.com

A Story and A Smile

Charles C. Fletcher

Published By
Fletcher Books
2310 Harris Circle NW
Cleveland, TN 37311

A Story And A Smile
Copyright © 2015 by Charles C. Fletcher

All rights reserved. No part of this book may be reproduced, stored in a retrieval system or transmitted in any form or by any means without the prior written permission of the publishers, except by a reviewer who may quote brief passages in a review to be printed in newspaper, magazine or journal.

The names used in this book are the inventions of the author who apologizes should he have inadvertently used the name of any actual person. No event or incident in the story is intended to relate to or represent any actual incident.

ISBN: 978-1-4951-4425-7
Published by Fletcher Books
2310 Harris Circle NW
Cleveland, TN, 37311

Printed in the United States of America

Contents

Medicine Show, 1930s 1
Teacher's Pet 7
An Airplane Ride 11
Biscuits and Gravy 14
Old Red and the Worm 19
Old Red and the New Rooster 22
Goodbye, Old Red 26
A Rooster for Dinner 31
As Time Goes By 35
Christmas, 1933 38
CCC Camp 46
Visit To CCC Camp 411 59
Wash Day, 1930s 70
Uncle Bob 77
My Dog And The Bob Cat 88
Saturday Night Bath 95
Neighbors 99
Preacher Bruce 105
Possum Dinner 109

JULY 4TH	117
ENGLISH VACATION	125
FOX HUNTING	133
WAL-MART COWBOY	139
TRADING COWS	142
MODEL 'A' FORD	149
HOG KILLING TIME	155
GRANDPA PRESSLEY	160

Forward

The stories in this book are hot related to each other and only a few are related to the same subject. The contents are from events and stories I heard while growing up in the mountains of Western North Carolina and in some slightly revised by events I observed or heard in the 80s and to my present age of 93.

Some of these stories you may remember from quotes of my books. The other I wrote from every day events I heard or saw. All events with references from a story are intended to bring a smile to your face.

I hope you enjoy these short stories and they bring a smile to you.

I write these stories so they will be documented for future generations after I am gone.

A Story and A Smile

Medicine Show, 1930s

Believe it or not, there was a lot of entertainment in the mountains and on the farms of Western North Carolina. And a lot of it was free, which was just fine for most all the local people of Canton and Haywood County.

The Medicine Show that came to Canton at least once a year was always a big draw. The Medicine Show was usually a group of four to five people. Of course, the main performer was called the "Doctor" or "The Medicine Man." Some even called him the "Con-Man." Regardless of what we called him, he was a pro. He usually owned the whole outfit, and the others were his employees.

I remember one Medicine Show better than the rest. They came to town and posted notices around town and on trees in the country announcing when and where the show would take place. Everyone had daily chores that had to be done. There was the milking and feeding the hogs, horses, and cows.

The notices gave those who were interested time to plan their schedules so they could attend. When the big day arrived, people hustled around and finished their evening chores, ate a quick supper, and hit the road to go see the Medicine Show. The dirty dishes from supper could be washed later.

The stage was already set up, all ready for the show to start. It was on the back of the Medicine Man's truck. The truck was used as a dressing room and to haul all the supplies and entertainers from town to town. Out the Medicine Man came from the back of his truck through the curtains hanging at the back of the stage. The Doc was the star of the show, all dressed up in his black suit and black bowtie.

"Welcome, ladies and gentlemen. Gather up close for some of the best entertainment you will ever see. Tonight we have the best one-man band in this entire country. He plays three musical instruments at a time. Ladies and gentlemen, welcome the one and only, Red Davis!"

Out Red Davis came with his guitar, drums, and harmonica. "What tune do you want him to play?" the Doc asked.

Requests came from every direction.

"Wait a minute," Doc said. "Red can play any tune you want, but he can't play them all at the same time. Tell you what, how about "Orange Blossom Special?"

Old Red was already playing, and some were clapping their hands and humming along. Doc was just getting the crowd in the mood for the real show.

Old Red played several songs on his instruments and sang one. He played his songs regardless of what the crowd asked for. When Old Red was finished warming up the crowd, he left his drums on the stage and went back into the truck. The curtains were hardly closed before a pretty young lady jumped out, dressed in brightly colored clothes with a blouse that left her belly bare and a short skirt nearly up to her knees. All the men folk stretched their necks and tried to get up closer. Many got a good elbow in the ribs from their wives.

"What I have to offer you tonight is one of the modern miracles of medicine. You children move back so mom and dad can get up close! Yes sir, this is the best medicine on the market today. When you buy from me, you have a 100% guarantee that it will do everything I say it will do."

"How many of you folks have aching backs, arms, legs, and other pains? How about that tired feeling after a hard day's work or a nagging headache? Folks, I have the answer to all your problems right here."

He turned to the young lady and said, "Mother would you hand me a couple of bottles of 'Chief Running Deer's Secret'? This medicine is made from roots, bark, and other secret ingredients straight from the woods of the Cherokee Indian Reservation. I am the only white man allowed to sell it. You children move back, let the grown folks come up close."

"My price for this miracle medicine is only fifty cents a bottle. But if you want to have a good supply for the winter, I will let you have three for a dollar. Friends, I will probably lose money, but I want to take a vacation and need to sell it all! You, my lucky friends, get a bargain. Red, Mother, and I are leaving in a few days. Better hurry! What I have will go fast, and there ain't no more outside the Cherokee Nation."

Out came a dollar from my mom's apron pocket. She handed it to Doc. "Mother, hand this fine lady three bottles of that miracle medicine. Who's next?"

There were hands everywhere with a dollar in them. Doc and his young assistant were really busy. The ones who bought the tonic headed toward home. Soon everyone was gone, and Doc and his crew started to pack everything into the truck. After a very good night, they were ready to move on.

When we arrived home, Mom had to wash the dishes that we left on the table hurrying to the Medicine Show. Mom hadn't been in the kitchen very long until she started singing. She usually hummed or sang when she was working, but this time she was really letting it come out.

"WHEN THE SAINTS GO MARCHING IN. WHEN THE…SAINTS GO…" ♪ ♪ ♪

"Mom? What's wrong with you?"

"Oh, I was pretty tired and had an aching back , so I took a good dose of the medicine. WILL THERE BE ANY STARS…." ♪ ♪ ♪

Mom was letting the music out, LOUD AND CLEAR. Dad went to the kitchen and asked Mom if he could see the medicine. He looked on the back of the bottle where the ingredients were listed: "50 % alcohol— 50 % spring water— Artificial coloring and flavoring— Patent applied for."

Now Dad was known to like a good drink of homemade whiskey ever so often. "Wonder if Doc has left yet? I need a few bottles of that medicine.

Can't ever tell when I'll get sick. Better hurry before he gets to the next county." And off he went.

Mom's singing was becoming louder. "THIS LITTLE LIGHT OF MINE…" Mom was feeling her best. That medicine really did work.

Next year there would be another "Medicine Show" coming to Canton but usually had a different Medicine Man. We didn't care who came. The entertainment was always good, and it was always free. Also, the medicine seemed to help the "sick" people. Hope he doesn't stay away too long.

Teacher's Pet

As I think back to the happy days in the new Beaverdam School, I realize many funny things happened too. And some not so funny. Here is one of those things and I don't know what category you would call it.

Back in the 1930s during the great depression a lot of poor people lived in the mountains of Western North Carolina. My family was some of those people. All of our family had to do their share in finding ways to have something to eat. We depended on whatever come our way.

I remember the many giant chestnuts that were on the mountains. Many were near a hundred feet high with a diameter of ten or more feet across the bottom. When they bloomed in the spring the mountains looked like they were covered with snow. Only the people near my age today ever saw this beautiful scene.

In the fall when the trees began to drop their fruit, the ground would be covered with shiny black nuts. Not only did the animals depend on them for food, people like me and my family made certain we collected our share.

Come Sunday noon after we finished our dinner (dinner is at noon and supper the evening meal to mountain people), my mom would give all us children one of her pillow slips and send us on our way to one of the many chestnut trees to gather their sweet black nuts. When we returned mom would put on a pan of water and boil some nuts. In the oven of the old wood stove she would make another batch.

Then came the part we were waiting for. Eating chestnuts. Let's get back to the school house and what happened the following Monday.

Beaverdam school was made from brick in 1932. Brick on the outside, wooden floors on the inside. Plenty of windows but no fans or air conditioning. Our heat for warmth in those bitter cold winters was from hot water flowing through big iron things along the wall we called radiators. Not much heat but better than what we were used to in the old one room school we first went to. For ventilation we would open the windows so the cool mountain air could come inside. On the cold days we never opened the windows.

I was in the fourth grade of school and we had the best teacher in Beaverdam school. A lady teacher by the name of King. We all called her Miss King.

I'm sure you know the gas and smell our digestive system makes when we eat certain foods like dried beans, sweet potatoes, and other foods but the granddaddy of them all is boiled chestnuts. Miss King was aware of the chestnut season and asked all her students to not eat them before or during the days we were in her class. Most of us did what she asked. No chestnuts while in school.

I sat behind the smartest student in the fourth grade. Her name was Betty. She made sure that I could see the answers when I didn't know them. With this arrangement I was a "A" student.

Betty had one bad habit. She loved to eat. There was always something hid in her desk that she would sneak and eat during the day. And this eating habit showed with Betty and her figure. She was a little on the plump side.

This day was one of those Mondays when everyone had been eating chestnuts and Betty had a passion for the sweetness of these nuts.

Miss King had assigned us our work that morning and it was as quite as a mouse in the class room. I glanced up and saw all the other students in class looking straight at me. That is everyone but Betty. Miss King walked up to my desk and didn't say a word. Just stood there with everyone staring and grinning at me.

I always took the blame if I had it coming but this wasn't my doing so I had to defend myself. In a low softy voice I said to my teacher, "Miss King, that wasn't me, I cooped my hand over my mouth and said to her. "Betty Potted."

The class was all laughing except Betty. She was on me like a jaybird tearing into me. Only Miss King saved me for a sure death. She held Betty and I headed to the back of the room. Miss King told Betty she could be dismissed for the rest of the day and I was promoted to a seat in the back of the room.

Betty came back to school on Tuesday. I lost my friend and the good grades I once made all from Betty's love of boiled chestnuts.

An Airplane Ride

The marvels of the future were beginning to appear daily in the 1930s, one of these being the airplane. Every so often a small plane would land in someone's cow pasture and offer rides to anyone that had a dollar.

There were more spectators than riders, all gawking and "ohms" "ahs" when the pilot did flips and spins. Some shut their eyes to keep from seeing these maneuvers. Well, little did I know that I would soon take my first airplane ride.

It was in the winter of 1935. That winter we had one of the biggest snow storms that western North Carolina had ever seen. Not only was there snow, but the temperature was below zero for several days.

About a week after the storm, it began to warm up, and everything was getting back to normal. Our nearest neighbor, Carroll Clark, food two of his largest steers dead. They had not been able to get to the barn during the storm and had frozen to death.

There wasn't any machinery to dig graves for them, so his plans were to drag the carcasses up to the foot of the mountain and let the buzzards eat them.

It so happened that Carroll's brother-in-law, Bill Cordell, came by and viewed the problem of moving the dead cattle.

"Say. Why don't we skin 'em' and sell the hides to the Swift Packing House in Asheville? They buy cow hides," he said to me.

"How much do you think we'd get for them?" I asked.

"At least five or six dollars," Bill said.

Bill was about eighteen years old—three years older than me. He also owned his own car. I guess this had something to do with him and me being good friends. I had to walk, otherwise.

Well, we started the skinning job. It wasn't easy. The steer carcasses were frozen stiff. This made the job of skinning harder than usual. It took the better part of a day to skin the two steers, but we didn't give up.

About three or four days later, the snow had all melted, and the weather warmed up. Bill decided that it was time to take the skins to Asheville and make some money. So, off we went to the packinghouse. We were on our way to becoming rich. We sold the two hides for five dollars: $2.50 for Bill and $2.50 for me. We were wealthy.

Bill said, "Now that we have some money, let's go out to the airport and take an airplane ride."

"Sounds good to me," I said.

So, off we went. We found one of the pilots and asked about the ride and the cost.

"Well, things are pretty slow, and I need to warm up my plane, so I'll give you two a ride for two dollars—one dollar each. Load up," he told us.

Within ten minutes everything on the ground looked real small. I was holding onto the seat really tight and was a little scared. "Do you boys want me to do a few loops?" the pilot asked.

"No!" we said. "Take us back down. We've had our money's worth."

It was many years later before I took another airplane ride, and it was on a larger plane.

Biscuits And Gravy

When you go to a fast food eating place for breakfast and order, "Biscuits and Gravy," do you ever think about what you are eating or where the ingredients came from? How much work do you think it took to make the flour for the biscuit and gravy?

If you should get egg and biscuits you would know where the egg came from. Or if it be sausage you would know that the sausage was from a hog.

Let us take a look from the beginning as to where we get the wheat flower to make the biscuits and gravy.

I don't know how far back in history where wheat was used for food. The word "Wheat " is mentioned 52 times in the old testament of the bible so I would guess that it has been around from the beginning of time. It is used for food for mankind and food for animals.

Threshing day every year was a big event for the farmers that had wheat for the threshers that came around in the late summer. The owner of the threshing machine in our area was a farmer by the name of Bud Harris. He and his son Jack would do the moving of the machine from farm to farm. The moving was done with a tractor with iron wheels that were near six feet in diameter with iron spikes on them. The "set-up" and keeping the thresher running was the Harris's job as owners. Most of the work was the responsibility of the farmer where the work was taking place. Bud would hire a couple of employees for measuring.

The grain as it came out of the thresher. The pay was usually twenty or twenty five cents an hour. The farmer would pay the same if he had to hire someone.

The big wheat growers in our community, "Thickety," were, Bud Harris, Wilson Medford, Tom Sorrels, Johnny Willis and every once in a while Alden Clark had a few stacks.

Sometimes it would take several days to finish at one farm.

The women of the neighborhood were a big part of "Threshing Day." The women from all the farms that were on the threshing schedule would get together where the workers were at. Their job was to feed all of the ones that were working with the threshing. This was no small task because there were a large number of workers.

All the men of the farms that were having threshing would help their neighbors until everyone had their wheat in the storage places. This was a big challenge for the women folks to keep these hungry men feed.

I was close to fifteen years old the summer I worked with the threshers. I was paid twenty cents an hour and had several different Job assignments. I cut binds and feed the wheat into the thresher. I helped measure the wheat as it came out of the machine. It requires two people to do the measuring, if the farmer was paying Bud with a tool we would measure seven parts for the farmer and the eighth part went to bud as pay. Some paid him with money. How much, I don't know. I also was on the straw stack helping with the stacking. This was done around a long pole that was set in a hole in the ground. Usually there were two people on the stack and we had to place it around the "Stack Pole" in a way to keep it from sliding off. We did this with pitch forks. The stack of straw, when finished had to be shaped so the water and snow would not stay on or soak into the straw. If it wasn't smooth with a finish that looked pretty, then the person who did the stacking didn't know how to make a straw stack.

At the end of the work day which was from daylight until dark, all the workers had to find some place to take a bath to get the dust and straw off his body. If some of the workers lived to far from where the work was taking place they would spend the night with the owner of that location.

Usually every one left and returned early the next day.

I have only explained briefly about all the hard work that was required to have the wheat for the flour. But in order to have flour the wheat had to be taken to a flour mill and be ground into the fine soft powder we call flour.

Then the cooks take over for making the biscuits and gravy that we have for breakfast. Their job also requires some skill. They have to know exactly how much of each ingredient to add and how long to cook it.

The biscuit is eaten with many other "Add-On's" but most of the time with the old stand-by, "Gravy."

The next time you eat breakfast and have the old stand-by as the main course, take a moment to think of all the hard work that it took so you could have...

BISQUITS AND GRAVY

Old Red And The Worm

One of the many places where we lived was in a house located up one of the deep hollows of Little Sam Mountain. There were no level places to build a house, so it was built on wooden poles. In this kind of mountainside house, the front was usually five or six feet high while the back was touching the ground. All the buildings were built to fit on a sloping hillside. This included the outside toilet. It was built from rough lumber. We had what you would call a deluxe model: it was a two-seater.

The "outhouse," as we called it, was a very popular meeting place for the womenfolk to sit and gossip. The men folk would use it for reading or simply as a resting place. Of course, it was also used for what it was built for.

We had an uncle who would visit pretty often, and the outhouse was his favorite place to relax and meditate. When asked why he stayed so long, he usually said he was reading about the latest farm equipment in the Sears Roebuck or Montgomery Ward catalogs that were always there. We used them for our toilet paper.

This was also a special building for Old Red, our Rhode Island Red Rooster. He was a very smart chicken and knew where all the good things in life were. He dearly loved worms as one of his favorite meals, and there was no better place to find them than under the outhouse. He would make a couple of trips there every day checking for worms.

Now, this uncle was visiting one day, and it just so happened that he and Old Red paid a visit to the outhouse at about the same time. Uncle was relaxed, catching up on his reading, and Old Red was checking out everything below, looking for the big fat worms. Red happened to look up. He batted his eyes, shook his head, and all at once he leaped up. Uncle let out a blood curdling scream, and out of the outhouse he ran trying to get his overalls on. Old Red now knew that what he had thought was a giant worm was not a worm after all. He to started running in a direction opposite from the way Uncle was going.

After Uncle regained his breath, he asked, "Where do you keep the shotgun? I'm going to kill that crazy rooster."

No one was about to help him. The whole family liked Old Red. He kept the farm yard safe for all the other animals. So, Uncle cut his visit short. He packed up and went to visit some of his other relatives, and Old Red came out of hiding. We all knew that we wouldn't be seeing this uncle again anytime.

Old Red And The New Rooster

Everything was going pretty good for Old Red, but he was getting older and had slowed down quite a bit. He no longer paid any attention to the capons, and he paid less attention to his family than before. The family had grown larger during the past year. There were all the old hens and ten new young pullets. There was also a young rooster along with several new young capons, and you could see that the young rooster was the son of Old Red. He was hatched in the early spring and had survived Dad's pocket knife surgery.

One day Old Red began to notice that there was a change taking place in his family. Nearly all the old hens and a few of the pullets began to hang out more with the young rooster. He had started crowing, but it was nothing like the sound Old Red made when he crowed. The young rooster was just getting started, and I guess you could say that his voice was changing. Anyway, this began to bother

Old Red. The young rooster would start crowing between four and five o'clock every morning, the way Old Red had done when he was young. Lately, Old Red would start crowing sometime after six o'clock in the morning.

The early crowing and the way the hens and pullets were acting began to be quite a concern for Old Red. He didn't like it at all, so he began to make plans to change a few things around the farm. He wanted things to be like they were before the new young rooster came along. He simply was not getting the attention he deserved or the respect he should be getting; after all, he was the chickens' protection from the cats, the dogs, and any other critter that came their way.

Old Red thought to himself, "I know what I'll do. I'll give that smart young rooster a good whipping, and that will put him back in his place."

This seemed to be an easy task to Old Red, but he had forgotten that he wasn't as young as he once was and that the young rooster was a lot quicker than he was. The young rooster wasn't as big or as heavy as Old Red, but he was a pretty smart bird after all, he was the son of Old Red.

One day the young rooster was scratching around looking for earthworms. He found one and began to cluck: "Cluck ... cluck-cluck" (chicken talk). Almost all of the hens and pullets ran to the young rooster. Old Red saw this, and the blood shot to his face. He decided right then and there to put a stop to this nonsense. He ruffled up his feathers and started toward the young rooster as fast as his legs would carry him. The young rooster saw him coming, but he didn't budge. He ruffled up his feathers and was ready to do battle with Old Red. He had a good thing going and was not about to give it up without a fight.

The young rooster glanced around and right away he new that Old Red was about to give him a good flogging. He jumped as high as he could, and Old Red scooted right under him. The first thing Old Red knew, the young rooster was sitting on his back and pecking and chewing his comb. Old Red regained his balance and was all over the young rooster. He started giving him a good flogging. The blood from his comb was running down into his eyes. This had never happened to Old Red before. Finally, the young rooster and Old Red decided to call the fight a draw. Each one began to slowly move away from the other. The old hens gathered around Old Red feeling sorry for him and clucking to tell him that they still liked him; but from that day on, it looked like the "Young Rooster" would be the big boss over our chicken flock.

Goodbye, Old Red

Well, things were going pretty smooth around the farm, especially with Old Red. He had decided to take an early retirement and let the young rooster handle all the daily chores. After all, he had watched over his family for more than three years. In the life of a chicken, this was a very long time.

As for the young rooster, all the hens were looking to him to supply all their daily needs and protect them from the other animals. This was a pretty big job for him because the number of hens in the flock had increased from eight to twelve. There were also the capons that the young rooster had to protect, but protection was all he gave them. He had no interest in where they went or what they did; he had all he could handle with the twelve hens. Also, the young pullets expected more attention from him than the old hens did.

Egg production had increased; more little chicks were being hatched; and my Dad started to notice the young rooster more. He began to start thinking: "Why are we keeping an old rooster when we don't need him? All he does is sit around in the shade and eat. He's getting so fast that he could have a heart attack. But, on the other hand, I don't think that any of the family, including me, could eat him if we decided to make a Sunday meal of chicken and dumplings. I've got to come up with a plan to get rid of Old Red."

Getting rid of Old Red was not as big a problem as Dad thought it would be. He was talking to a neighbor who lived up the hollow from where we lived, and it so happened that he, too, had the same problem that we had. He had an extra rooster to get rid of, and no one in his family wanted to eat him.

"Why don't we just trade roosters," Dad said. "I'll give you Old Red for your rooster and a half bushel of corn."

"Why do you want me to give you my rooster and the corn?" the neighbor asked.

"Well, Old Red is a lot larger than your rooster, and he is as fat as mud. Your rooster will have to be put in a coop and fattened up before we can eat him," Dad told him.

"All right. It's a deal," the neighbor agreed. "I'll bring my rooster over tomorrow and get your old red rooster." Everything was working out pretty well with getting rid of Old Red.

It so happened that, in about three weeks, the circuit-rider preacher would be coming to hold the annual three week revival meeting at the local Baptist Church. This preacher had to be fed and given a place to sleep during the time he would be here for the revival. Of course everyone knows that a Baptist revival preacher's favorite food is chicken. He doesn't care how you cook it as long as you have it at meal time and there is enough to have a second helping.

To get your name mentioned and be praised for what a fine meal you served before the preaching started, you had to have the preacher over to your house for a meal. The womenfolk very much liked to get this recognition. Seeing who could get their names mentioned during a revival meeting was sort of like a contest to them. They wanted to be able to brag about all the compliments they got from the preacher about their chicken, their apple cobbler, their biscuits, and all the other good food they had on the table when the preacher came to their house for dinner.

We had never had a preacher come to have dinner with us. I guess it was because my Mom didn't think that she could compete with the other women because we never had a chicken that we could spare for the preacher's dinner. But now, trading Old Red had given us our first chance to feed the preacher. Mom was all excited about it, and she began to plan a meal like we had never seen in our whole lifetime. She meant to see to it that the preacher would really brag on her cooking.

The time finally came. We were to feed the preacher on the second Sunday of the revival meeting. Things were really buzzing around the house. Everyone had to keep out of the way so Mom could get everything ready.

The preacher was ready to eat as soon as he got to our house. After he said a long prayer blessing the food, we were all ready to eat. The preacher got first choice of the food. Mom had cooked the most chicken and dumplings we had ever seen. She had added extra milk and a lot of extra dumplings to the Windot rooster. After eating several helpings of chicken and dumplings and apple cobbler, the preacher burped real loud and said, "This is the finest meal I've ever had. I think I'll go upstairs and take a short nap before the services begin."

I guess this was the day that Mom had been looking forward to. She was really happy, and all of this was made possible by Old Red. He had supplied the chicken and dumplings for Mom's special meal.

A Rooster For Dinner

The revival meeting was over, the preacher was gone, and there were a lot fewer chickens in the hollow than there were before the revival. This reduction in the chicken population included the departure of Old Red, too. Feeding the revival preacher also took its toll of capons. (The smart ones had hid out in the woods until everything got back to normal.) Our family enjoyed the great meals we had during the revival because we usually only ate vegetables and corn bread. Chicken on the table was for special occasions only.

Everything around the farm was back to normal. The young rooster had calmed his flock down, and they were over their nervous spell. The egg production was getting better, and the young rooster was getting cockier everyday. Sometimes he would attempt to flog and fight some of the family. He wasn't afraid of anything. He was also venturing out of his territory.

Wherever we lived in the mountains of Western North Carolina, we kept our house cool in the summer months by leaving all the windows and doors open. This would let the cool air from the mountains flow through the house. We could regulate the temperature of the house by opening or closing the windows and doors.

At this time, we were living in a house in Buckeye Cove, near Canton, North Carolina. One day, Mom had our mid-day meal on the dinning table. For some reason, she had to leave the room for a few minutes. It so happened that the young rooster was on the back porch at the time. I don't know if a rooster can smell or not, but, just the same, this one spotted the food on the table and also noticed that there was no one around. Into the house he went. With one big jump, he was on the table. Once there, he began to help himself to our dinner.

When Mom came back and saw what was taking place, she let out a yell and made a dive for that rooster. Down from the table he hopped; then he ran out the back door and to the barn as fast as he could go.

When we came in to eat lunch, Mom told us what had happened. I began to plan what to do because I figured that this was not the last time for a visit from that rooster. I got me a large "poke" (a paper bag), a hand full of dried beans, and some string. I put the dried beans into the poke and then blew air into the poke. When it was full of air, I tied it real tight. It looked sort of like a basketball. I was ready for that rooster when he "came to dinner" again.

Sure enough, a couple of days later, here he comes. Mom and I hid so he couldn't see us. Up, onto the table he went. I ran around the house and shut the door so he couldn't escape. Then I grabbed him by the legs, took him outside, and tied the bean-filled poke to one of his legs. I turned him loose, and he started running. The bean bag was following right behind him. He stopped and began to try to fight whatever it was that was following him. He made a terrible racket. Whenever he turned, so did his enemy. There was nothing he could do but to try to run away from it; but he couldn't outrun it. Soon, he was so tired that he gave up and fell over on the ground.

I figured he had learned a lesson, so I cut the string and removed the poke. After a few minutes he got his wind back and decided to run some more. Off he went, and he noticed that there wasn't anything chasing him. He stopped, flapped his wings, put his head as high as he could, and crowed the loudest he had ever crowed. He was telling everyone that he had won the fight. Be that as it may, from that day on, that rooster never came into the house for dinner again.

As Time Goes By
1930–2015

As I become closer to my 94th birthday I think back at the way boys and girls changed the way they dressed and acted back then and today in what we call "modern times."

As an example we will take a look at the way the girls dressed in 1930 and today the year 2015.

When the girls in the sixth and higher grades began to grow toward young women they would stoop there head and shoulders down to keep the young men from noticing them.

As all of the people in the early days we were poor. We boys didn't do much to improve our appearance but the girls did what they could with the clothing they had. They didn't have underclothes to change the shapes of their body.

Today in our modern time the girls begin to show as much flesh as they can without being taken to jail. When I say, "the girls" they start as young as ten years old and all the way up too seventy or older.

I don't consider myself one to lust on women but after all I am a man and notice women and how they dress.

I have seen many funny things in my long lifetime. Some I liked and some I didn't like.

If you have been to WALMART you have seen the young and old females that dress like what they think is up to date and modern.

WALMART is a very nice place to shop and they have everything you need. I shop there quite often.

Just recently I needed a few groceries so off I go to shop. WALMART does have some faults as all places do. If you notice there are fourteen nice checkout stations but only four are in use and they all are marked 10 items only.

I buy my items and get in what I think is the shortest line.

This was my lucky day. Directly in front of me was a very beautiful girl I would guess about twenty one years old and she was dressed in the latest style. Low cut clothes, top and bottom. "WOW," Mother Nature sure had been good to that girl.

As she placed her items on the check-out belt I couldn't keep my eyes off her. Everything was unloaded from her cart except 10 pounds of Idaho baking potatoes. They were on the bottom shelf of the buggy. This is when the unexpected happened.

She bent over and took hold of the bag of potatoes to place them up front.

"POP', something broke loose. She didn't move. She was looking up at me, saw me standing there with eyes and mouth wide open.

"Well?" she asked me.

I had to think fast. I looked down at her and said, "Lady, if you would like to get rid of them two puppies you have in your arm, I'll take the one with the brown nose."

I ran for my life to a hiding place at the back of the store. I peeped around and she was gone. It was safe to pick up my groceries and go home.

CHRISTMAS, 1933

You will have to be in your 80s or close your eyes real tight to get a picture of what a Christmas was really like in the years of the "Great Depression." There was no going to the store and buying the things that you would need to decorate the house or a Christmas tree. Although we were very poor, we always managed to find a way to brighten up the house and get into the happy mood for Christmas. The following is a true account of what took place at our house when the Christmas season rolled around back then. I may miss a little or add to the actual things that took place because it was a very long time in the past. After all, I am 85 years old.

We would start getting ready for Christmas in the late fall when the chinquapins started opening. I am sure that anyone under the age of 60 doesn't know anything about a chinquapin. It is a relative of the chestnut. Instead of being a tree like the chestnut, it is a shrub-like bush about five feet tall.

The burrs and nuts look like those of a chestnut, but they are smaller, there is only one nut in each burr. Chinquapins were very plentiful in the 1930s in the mountains of Western North Carolina. They usually were found on the lower hillsides, not at the higher elevations like the chestnuts. They are all gone now along with the native chestnut trees. We would gather the small chinquapins and let them dry. They would become a part of our Christmas tree decorations when the time came to put up a tree for Christmas.

We could tell that it would not be long until Christmas when Mom would say, "You'd better be good because Santa Claus is watching you." My brother, TJ and I didn't really believe in Santa, but our two sisters who were lots younger thought that Santa was real. Anyway, we went along with the Santa thing. We would wish for a lot of things, but we knew that we would not be getting them because there was no extra money around the house.

Also, we knew that it would not be long until Christmas when the two churches in our area would begin to get their Christmas programs together. There was the Baptist church that we attended and the Methodist church. They would plan their programs so that everyone could attend both programs.

We were all neighbors, and we all shared the things that happened in our community. It would be nice if everything was the same today.

The church leaders would ask the children to do the acting in the Christmas plays. Usually it would be the young girls of the church who acted all the parts. We boys were a little shy, and, besides, the older boys would tease us if we took part in anything that included girls. The plays were put on at about the same time every year. Their theme was the birth of Christ, and that would never be changed. After all, this was, and still is, what Christmas is about. The womenfolk of the church would go all out to decorate the church. Their decorations were always pretty and original. Nothing was "store bought"; everything was "handmade."

Mom began planning what we were going to have for Christmas dinner. This meal was one of very few at which we were to have some sort of meat to go along with the canned beans and the potatoes from the cellar. We would also have sweet potatoes, big biscuits ("cat heads"), thick milk gravy, and, of course, one of Mom's special stacks cakes. These cakes were made with home-made cane syrup and cooked dried apples. They were about ten or twelve layers high. If some of our neighbors killed a beef, we would have stew beef for the meat. We could get this because it cost about 10¢ a pound. If we were not having beef, we would eat a goose that we would buy from Bert Robinson. He was the janitor at the Beaverdam School. The price for a goose was somewhere from 50¢ to $1. — it depended on how large the goose was.

At one week before Christmas, it was time to go get a Christmas tree. Getting a tree was TJ's and my job. We would get an axe, and off to the woods we would go. This was not a very hard job because there were plenty of pine and spruce trees to choose from. The tree had to be about five feet tall with plenty of limbs on it.

While we were out looking for the Christmas tree, the girls were busy with their job of getting the decorations ready for the tree. They strung the chinquapins using a darning needle and thread. These strings of chinquapins were garlands for hanging on the tree. The girls would make paper rings out of different colored paper that Dad had brought from the paper mill. These, too, would be put together to make a paper chain to hang on the tree.

Next came a fun part for Mom and the girls. Sometimes TJ and I would help, too. We would pop a couple of large pans of popcorn and make the popcorn into long strings. After we made the strings of popcorn, we dyed them different colors. This was done by dipping the strings of corn into different natural dyes. We used pokeberry to make a red dye. We made a brown dye from walnut hulls. We got a green dye from the bark of several types of trees.

After we had made and hung all our decorations, we would make a star from cardboard and place it in the top of the tree. Everything was now in place, and we had one of the prettiest Christmas trees in the entire community.

Next came the hanging of the stockings on the fireplace mantle. This was not an easy job because we usually didn't have any "socks." We wore our shoes without any socks. After searching through the house, we would each find a sock to put above the fireplace, even if wasn't one of our own.

The week before Christmas, we attended the Christmas programs at the two churches in our community. This was the time of the year when all the children would go to church. For a lot of them, this was the only time that they attended church for the entire year. They wouldn't miss this because after the program there was a treat for all the young children. It usually wasn't much — a couple of sticks of candy or an orange. This was a big treat for most of us because we didn't get candy or oranges very often.

On Christmas Eve everyone was excited. We would go to bed a lot earlier than usual. Santa Claus could come at any time, and if anyone was up and about in the house, he might fly on by and not stop. We would be lie really quiet in bed listening for the bells on his sleigh. We would try to stay awake as long as we could so that we might hear Santa coming to our house.

On Christmas morning we children were the first ones to get out of bed and go into the "sitting room" where the tree and our stockings were. Presents would be under the tree. Some were in brown paper bags; some were wrapped in white butcher's paper. They each had names on them.

The girls opened their gifts first. The youngest was first. Her name was on one of the white packages, and she began tearing the paper off it. Inside were a pretty new dress and some underwear. Then it was the next girl's turn. She tore off the paper wrapping on her present, and would you believe it — she also had a new dress and some underwear. I don't know if they were "store bought" or if Mom had made them from flour sacks. (Our flour came in cloth bags with beautiful prints on them, or you could get white ones. Nothing was wasted during those hard times.)

Next, it was time for TJ and me to open our brown paper bags. TJ was first; he had a new pair of denim pants and a blue cotton shirt. Then, I opened my bag, and I got the same things as TJ — pants and a shirt. This was great. We always got a new pair of overalls. We were getting older, and we wanted to dress differently from the "little boys."

Then we went directly to the fireplace to check our stockings. Each one had the same things in it: a couple of sticks of candy, an apple, and an orange. The dresses, pants, and shirts were forgotten now.

"Don't you kids eat any of that yet!" my mother hollered. "You'll spoil your breakfast, and we have a good one this morning."

We went to the long wooden table where there were hot biscuits, fried eggs, milk gravy, apple sauce, and home-made country sausage that Mom had canned when we killed a hog last fall. This sure was great eating. We finished eating and off we went to get at that candy. Soon it was dinner-time, and we went back to the long table for another special Christmas meal.

It would be another year before this would take place again. We were all happy; no one was sick; we had enough to eat; and, most of all, we loved each other. We were thankful for what we had. During these hard times in the early 1930s, a lot of people had less than we did.

CCC Camp

My uncle Clifford (my mother's youngest brother) and I had discussed the possibility of going into the Civilian Conservation Corps (CCC) Camps. This also was one of the New Deal projects started by President Roosevelt. There were around 1300 Camps around the country, twenty being in the Great Smokey Mountains. The Camps were set up to provide jobs for thousands of unemployed young men. Men between the ages of 17 and 25 who were unmarried, out of school, and unemployed were eligible. The pay was $30.00 a month. The men got $5.00, and $25.00 was sent home to their families. If a person had no family, the money was held in an account until his discharge from the CCC.

The CCC hired local experienced men to teach the Camp crews how to do the jobs they were assigned to do. Each Camp also had Army officers responsible for day-to-day operations. All the men were given clothing, shelter, and food in addition to their pay. At this time, the Army was feeding their men for 45¢ a day. The CCC men were allowed $1.50 a day for food. We got three good meals every day.

The work of the CCCs was a variety of jobs. They built telephone lines, roads, and bridges, planted trees, fought forest fires, stocked streams with fish, cut stone for walls, ran nurseries to grow tree seedlings, and did many other things. They had instructors to teach trades to anyone that wanted to learn a trade.

Clifford and I hitched a ride on a slow freight train to Waynesville from Canton. We went to the county courthouse to sign up for the CCC. We were given a date for the next selection of enrollees. We were to be at the courthouse no later than eight AM on the appointed day to leave for Camp. About thirty of us got into the back of an Army truck and set off. None of the enrollees knew where we were going.

About two hours later we were unloading at a Camp in Round Bottoms near the Cherokee Indian reservation. I believe the camp was called Ravensford. They fed us a very good lunch. Most of us had never seen so much food and so many different kinds of it. After lunch they began the process of choosing the men they wanted to keep. They only had room for twenty new people. Uncle Clifford was a big stout boy. I weighed maybe one-hundred pounds. They kept Clifford and sent me back to Waynesville along with nine others. We were promised that we would be on the next month's list. I sure was let down. I wanted to be with my uncle.

I reported for the next month's trip. Again, we were told only that we were going to a CCC Camp but not where. After a pretty long ride, the truck stopped, and we were told to get out. None of us recognized the place. We were told that the Camp number was 411 and that the place was Smokemont (the Kephart Camp). They kept all of us as enrollees. They explained the rules that we were to follow. They told us we were not to get any clothing until we had stayed one week. At that time khaki uniforms would be issued to us. Then they assigned us to a barrack like building.

On Monday morning right after breakfast everyone gathered at the Park Office for work assignments. All work assignments were given by Forest Service personnel. I was to go with the rock cutting crew. Our workplace was at a location along Highway 411 near a rock quarry.

The supervisor would have a large piece of rock placed on a table. He took a rule and did some measuring, made lines on the rock with a piece of chalk, and then said something like, "I want this stone to be x inches long and y inches wide and z inches deep with all sides as smooth as you can make them." He then handed me a large hammer and a couple of chisels, telling me, "When the chisels get dull, holler and someone will bring you some sharp ones."

There I was, in the hot sun, wearing a blue denim shirt and pants. I did not have a hat. I was wearing all the clothes that I owned. Sweat was pouring off this one-hundred pound boy. I had cut places on my arms and face, and I was working hard trying to show them I could take it. I was glad when that day was over. I was tired, sore, and hungry. The hungry part was soon gone because we had a very good supper. I took a good shower and went straight to bed.

This kept up for the whole week. I was getting more cuts and bruises. Also, my only clothes were dirty and beginning to get holes in them. I made myself a promise: come Saturday, (no work on Saturday or Sunday) I was going "over the hill" (going home) and not coming back. Saturday morning I got up at five while everyone in the barracks was asleep and headed down the mile long road to Highway 411 going toward Cherokee.

One of the rules of the Camp was never to hitch-hike or beg a ride from anyone. I was walking down Highway 411 long before daylight, when out of nowhere came a green pickup truck. I stuck out my thumb. I was desperate. I had to get out of those mountains. At that time there were lots of wild animals in the mountains. The truck stopped. It was still dark, and I didn't see who was giving me a ride.

"What are you doing up here in these mountains at this time of the day?" the driver asked.

"Well, I was in that CCC Camp up there, but I'm going home, and I ain't coming back."

"What's the problem?" he asked.

"I can't take that rock quarry. Look at the cuts and bruises on my face and arms. Lots of dust got in my eyes. We didn't have goggles. I don't mind working long, hard days, but I can't take that quarry."

It was getting light now, and I saw that the man who was driving was wearing green clothes. This bothered me. I knew that he belonged to the US Forest Service. He said, "Son, my name is J.O. Rosser. I'm the Park Superintendent from headquarters at Gatlinburg. If you will come back on Sunday and report for duty, I promise you that you will never go back to the rock pit again. What do you say?"

"I don't know. I'll have to think it over," I said.

We talked about other things until we were at Waynesville. "This is as far as I go," he said. "I'm going to a fire camp up at Catalooch. See you Monday."

"Maybe," I said.

I had to walk from Waynesville to Canton because there weren't many cars on the road, especially on Saturday. There wasn't much to do around home that weekend. Everyone seemed to have something to do except me. Come Sunday noon, I decided to go back to camp. I had pride; I wasn't a quitter; I'd show them.

I got a ticket and boarded the Trail way bus that went to Knoxville by way of Gatlinburg. The bus stopped on 441 where the road to the CCC Camp was. I made it in time for supper. I never got food this good at home. This was one of the things that brought me back.

Monday morning I reported to the park office where all the work assignments were given out. Everyone had left for work but me. I stood there, and the Park Supervisor motioned for me. I went to him, and he said, "Son, from now on your job will be to help out in the Park Office. You'll issue tools and keep records of who gets gas and how much they get and also have them sign for the gas." He knew my name. I guess Mr. Rosser told him because he had asked me my name on our ride to Waynesville on Saturday.

One of the perks of this job was that I moved into the Office bedroom. The reason for this is that I would have to answer the phone if any fires or emergencies were reported and make contact with the ones who needed to know about them. I shared this duty with the Park Clerk who also had to be on duty 24 hours each day. During the day when nothing was going on, I would practice driving the road graders and army trucks that were at the Camp. Things were not so bad after all. I'm glad I went back.

Our company was supervised by two Army officers, a captain by the name of Miller and a 1st lieutenant whose name I've forgotten. Everyone liked the Captain because he was like one of us. He didn't try to push us too far. This wasn't true with the Louie. He was sort of a smart-aleck who liked to show his authority.

As with most CCC Camps there were many mountain boys who would only take so much pushing and then they would do some getting even. This happened to the Lieutenant several times. As in the Army, we had to "sack our beds," so the officers' beds were sacked also. One night after "lights out," there was a scream from the officers' quarters. It was the Louie. Somehow, a great big black snake had found a sleeping place between the tightly stretched sheets on his bed. He called a meeting, but no one knew anything about that snake, and besides everyone claimed to be scared to death of any kind of snake. Everyone went back to bed with a grin on his face — that is, except the Lieutenant.

Another time, when all the workers came to Camp for dinner (lunch), they left the Mess Hall and all sat down on the rock wall in front of the barracks instead of reporting to the Park Office to be taken back to work. The officers were called; they had us all go to the Recreation Hall. The Captain wanted to know what the problem was. The spokesman for the CCC boys told the Captain that there wouldn't be anymore work until the food got better. It was the duty of the Lieutenant to purchase all supplies. He bought all the food locally in

Bryson City or Sylva and had been buying cheap meat and vegetables.

The Captain promised that he would personally promise that the food would be better. He then asked, "Is there anyone here who's hungry?"

A boy by the name of Forgy spoke up: "I am," he said.

Now, old Forgy was an over-sized mountain boy who was our Fire Watch and took care of the generators that supplied our electric power for lighting. The cooks had joined the meeting, also. The Captain whispered something to the Head Cook, and he left. He soon returned with a large box of soda crackers (saltines) and a gallon tin can of Vienna sausages. The Captain told the Cook to give this to Forgy. He took both the crackers and sausages, sat down at a table and began eating. Everyone left to go back to work except Forgy. When the last one left, Forgy was still eating his crackers and sausages.

My friend Forgy met with the Captain again later on. As mentioned, he was Fire Watch, so his job was at night. He usually slept pretty much in the day time. He also could go to the Mess Hall whenever he wanted to eat, and the cooks would feed him.

One day while at the mess hall eating, he heard a lot of noise out back of the Mess Hall. He went to find out what was going on. There were several black bears eating out of the garbage cans. One of the smaller bears was inside of an overturned can. Forgy took the lid of the can and shoved the bear inside, put the lid on the can, turned it up, and sat on the top.

"Go get the captain! Go get the captain!" Forgy hollered.

Someone told the Captain that Forgy needed to see him out behind the mess hall. The Captain walked out back and saw Forgy sitting on top of the garbage can.

"What do you want," he asked?

"Cap, I've got a bear in this can. Take your gun and shoot through the side and kill him. I'll skin him, and the cooks will cook him, and we'll have bear for dinner tomorrow.

"Get off that can and let that bear go," ordered the Captain.

"But bear meat is really good eating, and I ain't had any since I left home," Forgy complained.

"Git." said the captain.

Forgy got off the can slowly, and the bear jumped out and headed for higher ground. Forgy returned to his eating. The Captain headed back to his quarters with a smile on his face wondering if there would be other meetings with his friend Forgy, the fire watchman.

As I mentioned, everyone liked the Captain. He had a small radio with about 100 feet of aerial that would let him get a station from St. Louis where the Cardinals baseball team was. He let us listen to the broadcast of the ballgames. We were all Cardinals fans.

Saturday was the day most everyone looked forward to. First thing was that there was no working, with the exception of necessary work such as that of the cooks, the Vehicle Checker (who checked cars entering and leaving the Smokeys), and a few others. Everyone else piled into the back of a truck and headed to the towns of Bryson City or Sylva for a recreation trip. We could see a movie if we had the dime for a ticket. Then there was the most important event, the Saturday night square dance. Even if you didn't dance, you always met a lot of pretty country girls. They, too, came out on Saturday for the same reason that the CCC boys did. They wanted to meet the CCC boys. Everybody was happy. Some of the older boys fell in love (so they said) and later married the girls they met.

One Saturday night I was taking my girl friend home. I asked her how far away she lived because the truck back to camp left at 11 PM, and if you weren't in the truck, they didn't wait for you. She told me it wasn't very far. So, off we went hand in hand, across foot logs, through the woods, and over fences.

I didn't have a watch, but something told me I had better head back to town, or I would be walking the 30 plus miles back to Camp. I said a quick goodbye, and here I went running as fast as I could in the dark. I soon saw the lights of town, and I thought if I was lucky I would make it. I just did get there in time. I was the last one getting on the truck. This was the last time I offered to take my dancing partner home.

We didn't spend much money on these trips, maybe a few nickels for soft drinks. We didn't have much money. Our five dollars a month pay didn't last very long. Most of it was spent in the Canteen at Camp for cigarettes and chewing tobacco.

I began to get a real education while in the CCCs. I learned how to take care of myself and how to get along with other people even though none of us ever thought alike. There were as many personalities as there were people. Even with our different ways of thinking, we were like a family. Everyone helped, and we looked out for each other. As I write this I keep thinking how things have changed since the days I was in the CCCs. We were poor in worldly possessions but rich in the way we treated each other. In other words, we were humble because we were all alike — we were all poor people.

The Visit To CCC Camp 411

Charles Fletcher
Clarence Allison

My phone rang — I picked up the receiver — "Hello...?"

"Charles, this is Clarence Allison.' I am planning to visiting the old 411 CCC camp site this weekend. Want to meet me at the gate where the road to the camp leaves the main road?"

I could meet you on Saturday about 10 AM. You know, it's been sixty eight years since I left the CCCs. I would guess that the camp is full of ghost by now. Could be spooks hanging around just waiting for someone like you and me to come back.

"I don't think so," I stopped by for a few minutes about a year ago. Didn't stay long. The foundations are still there and the rock wall in front of the barracks is still standing. I'll meet you at the gate at ten next Saturday morning. Bring a couple of sandwiches and something to drink and we will stay all day.

Between the two of us we should remember where all the buildings were. I'm sure it will bring back a lot of memories along with some stories and what we did nearly seventy years ago. "Good bye, see you Saturday morning."

CCC camp 411 at Smokemont was located near the Cherokee Indian reservation in the Smokey Mountain National Park in North Carolina.

Clarence was one of the cooks at this camp. He was only sixteen years old when he reported for duty. They would ask, "how old are you?"

Whatever you told them was your age. Your age was never checked . Most of the young men didn't have a birth certificate. They were born at home with a midwife acting as the doctor. Their birth was recorded in the family bible.

When I arrived at the gate across the road leading to the abandoned CCC camp. Clarence was waiting for me. I parked off 441 highway beside Clarence.

"Do you think we can walk the half mile to where the camp was?" I said to Clarence.

We are not as young as we were seventy years ago. We are old men now, you being eighty one and me eighty seven,. May have to rest a couple of times along the way.

The first foundation we came to was where the mess hall was located. This was Clarence's work place.

"Eat many a good meal in the building that was on that foundation," I said to Clarence. Brings back lots of memories.

"Sure does," Clarence said. I learned to drive a truck behind the mess hall. One of the truck drivers really loved milk. He would drink all he could get and want more. I would sneak bottles of milk out of the refrigerator for him and in return he would leave his truck behind the mess hall for me to practice my driving.

"Do you remember the time that John Forgy caught the bear in back of the mess hall?" I asked Clarence.

"Sure do, John was always doing crazy things. I don't know how he caught that bear."

"I do."

You remember that John was the night watchman and he slept most of the day. He would come to the mess hall when he woke in the evening and you would feed him.

You remember how the bears were always in the garbage cans searching for food. Well — this one evening when John came to the mess hall he noticed a big cub bear all the way in one of the garbage cans. John sneaked up behind the can with the cub inside, picked up a lid, slammed it on the can, turned it up and sat on the top. He had caught himself a bear.

Go get the Captain—Go get the Captain John was hollering.

Someone got word to the Captain and he came to where John was setting on the garbage can.

"What do you want?" he asked.

"Captain—I've got a bear in this can. You shoot him with your pistol, kill him and we'll have a bear dinner."

"You get your butt off that can and let that bear go."

If I killed that bear we both would be sent to prison.

We did other things trying to keep the bear out of the garbage but nothing worked. They kept coming back.

A little ways up the road from the mess hall on our left was the rock wall that was in front of our barracks. This was where we sat in the evenings to rest after a hard days work.

"That second foundation is where my barrack was," I said to Clarence.

"I was in the first one, guess they wanted me close to the mess hall," Clarence said.

I remember when a boomer got in our barrack. Not may people know what a boomer is. They belong to the squirrel family. Not as large as a gray squirrel and larger than a ground squirrel. A boomer is the fastest animal in all the of these mountains. When we threw something at him he would be in the other end of the barrack before it left your hand.

After throwing shoes and anything we could get our hands on we gave up and opened the doors in the barrack and he left .

Also got my bed tied up in the ceiling one time when I went to Bryson City one Saturday night to the square dance. I didn't complain and it never happened again.

Over there was where Forgy had the generator that he started every night. That building next to the generator house was the training building where you could learn a trade if you wanted to.

The other building on our right was the canteen and recreation hall. We didn't have much money to spend at the canteen. We were paid thirty dollars a month. Five for us and the other twenty five was given to our family. We were glad for the twenty five dollars to go to our family. This helped send the younger children to school and support our family in many ways.

Over there was where the army officers had their offices and bed rooms. We had a captain and a lieutenant. Everyone in camp liked the captain but the lieutenant was fresh out of officers training and liked to show his authority. He didn't have to many friends.

"Clarence, do you remember that someone had to make the officers' beds and they had to be 'sacked?' And do you remember when someone put a live five-foot black snake in the lieutenant's bed and after he recovered from the shock he called a meeting in the recreation hall trying to find out who the snake handler was?" The rumor was that from that day on he would never get in bed without removing the sheets and blankets.

A little farther up the road we came to where the park office was. "This was where I worked," Charles said.

Let me tell you how I got this job.

The first week in camp I was assigned to the rock cutting crew. For some reason I was not issued work clothes. May have been because I was so skinny or they wanted to see if I was staying.

The crew leader would have a large stone placed on a table. I was given a big hammer and a chisel and told to make the bolder a certain size by chipping it. When Friday finally came I was cut all over my arms and face from flying chips from the stone. I had a plan. Come Saturday I was leaving this place.

Early Saturday morning I slipped out of the barrack. Walked down the road to 441 highway going to Cherokee. I was walking as fast as I could go. I was scared because there was lots of wild animals in these mountains.

Out of nowhere the lights from a car came up behind me. After passing me it stopped. When I was closer I could see that it was a green park truck. A voice from inside the truck asked. "What are you doing in these mountains at this time of the day?"

I was really scared but managed to answer. I was in that CCC camp but I am going home and not coming back.

"Where is your home, he asked?"

"Canton," I said.

"Get in, I'm going to Waynesville, that's pretty close." I got in the truck and we were on our way to Waynesville when the driver asked, "Why are you leaving the CCC camp?"

I've been cutting rocks all this week and I have cuts all over my body, I can't do this kind of work .

"My name is Ross Eaken*, I am the park superintendent here. If you will come back Monday I promise that you will not have to work in the rock quarry again."

"I'll think about it."

Things were kind of boring around home on Saturday and Sunday morning. I was kind of missing some of the boys I had become friends with and most of all the good food that we had every meal and plenty of it. I decided to go back.

I walked to town, bought a ticket and was on the Trailways bus going back to camp.

On Monday morning I went to the park office where all the work was assigned for that day. Every one was given a job and had left, I was still waiting when one of the park employees told me that I was to help out in the park office, issue tools and put gas in the park rangers trucks.

I was to keep a record of who checked out tools and have the drivers sign for the gasoline they got.

The park office clerk was a boy from some where in Tennessee. He answered to the name of Rod. He explained the office duties to me and how to recognize the different rings on the phone. This was the first time I had ever talked on a phone. It was a little spooky to talk with someone that were miles away.

Another good thing happened. I moved into the park office from the barrack. Someone had to be near the phone around the clock in case there was a call for help from an accident or a fire report. Rod and I had a bed room in the back of the office.

Everything good was going my way. Rod had a small radio and with the help of several hundred feet of wire strung thru the trees we could hear the baseball games from St. Louis and the Grand Old Opera from Nashville, Tennessee on Saturday night.

I am glad that I came back to camp 411.

"Clarence, did you look at the old fish hatchery place when you were here?"

"Yes, the building is gone but several of the fish ponds are still there."

"Do you remember when some of the boys would slip in the building and steal some of the big trout that were kept for spawning?"

"Yes, They would get them cooked by someone in the mess hall. I never did cook any for them."

"It's a pretty long walk up there and we are many years older so we will skip the hatchery," I said.

As we were walking back to our car on the exit road that was back of where the barracks use to be Clarence pointed to a big hole in the ground.

"Do you know what that is?" he asked.

"I believe that is where the septic tank was for our sewage system."

"You are right, Clarence said." The man that was a crew leader and the dynamite man at the rock quarry designed and supervised building the tank.

As we approached the place where we had left our cars I said to Clarence."

"I'm glad that you called me and invited me to visit "The old 411 CCC camp." Sure brought back memories of "the good old days." I didn't realize when I enlisted in the CCC's that what I learned would help make me a better citizen, soldier, employee and father. The money that we receives was not the important part of our growing up from a poor young boy in these mountains to a young man with responsibilities and the desire to help our fellow man. I am proud to tell others that I was a part of President Roosevelt's "Tree Army," the CCC's.

"Good bye Clarence," thanks for the invitation to visit 411 with you.

NOTE:
* Ross Eakin was the first park superintendent, serving from January 1931 until 1945.

Wash Day, 1930s

If the words, "wash day" were mentioned today, in 2013, very few people would know what you were talking about. Only the "Old-timers" like me and a few of the younger generation who heard about it from their grandfathers or some other person who grew up back in the 1920s and 1930s would know.

Wash day was usually on the same day every week. This was usually on a Monday and lasted through Tuesday, and for a Very large family it would be sometime Wednesday before it was completed.

Wash day as we know it today means turning some dials, pushing a button, and adding some washing detergent. There is no certain day for this now. Only when the modern, automatic washer is loaded with dirty clothes do we do the laundry.

There Are no outside clothes lines for drying the washing? We just move the clothes from the washer to the dryer and push another button. We sit down, read a book, or watch TV until the buzzer sounds telling us the drying are completed.

Very few of the things that we wash are never ironed. Most everything is "wash & wear."

This means that there are no wrinkles and the crease is the same As before washing. Even with all these conveniences, we often hear, "I dread tomorrow. It's wash day."

Let me tell you what took place on wash day when I was growing up in the 1930s and early 40s. The day for wash day was always decided by the woman of the home. This was the way it should be because she did most of the work and sometimes all of it. The woman of the house would have the older boys cut the fire wood and fill the boiling pot and the rinsing tubs with water. This was done the night before or early on wash day before leaving for school.

I'm thinking that Monday was chosen for wash day because the only relaxation and rest the women got was on Sunday afternoon after the Sunday dinner was finished. Usually there was no cooking on Sunday night? We had to eat whatever was left over from the noon meal if there was anything. There was usually an extra cake of corn bread that we could eat with cool glass of milk from the spring box. The spring box was where the milk, butter, or any other food that needed to be kept cool was stored. As with the washing machines today, there were no refrigerators then. Even if there had been any of these conveniences, we couldn't have used them. There was no electric power in the communities around the mountains of Western North Carolina. Only the city folks had electric lights.

The electrical gadgets, as we called them, were not invented at this time of the 20th Century. Later in the 30s there was hand cranked clothes wringers for us country people and the ones for those who had electricity were turned by an electric motor.

Now, back to wash day at our house. The wood was cut for the fire to boil the clothes in the big cast iron pot. All the rinse tubs (three) and the boiling pot were filled with water from the spring or the hand dug well. The source depended on where we were living. At one place we lived the well was close to one hundred feet deep. We would lower a bucket tied to a rope and bring up the water. It took some time to fill the pot and tubs.

I or my brother TJ would start the fire around and under the big iron boiling pot. After this we went off to school.

Mom was On her own. As soon as it was light enough, here came Mom With the first load of clothes to be washed. She had sorted the white things from the colored. Whites were always the first to be washed. She had a washing stick about five feet long. This was for placing the clothes in the boiling water, stirring them while boiling, and moving them to the first rinsing tub.

The pot was loaded and next to be added was a bar of homemade soap. This was made at hog killing time. It consisted of the excess fat from the hog mixed with caustic lye made from the ashes of wood. This strong soap along with the boiling removed any dirt or stains from the things being washed.

Mom didn't have a watch to time the boiling, but she knew the correct boiling time and would remove them with the washing stick. This stick helped mom do two things with her washing.

First, she didn't have to get too close to the fire and risk getting her clothes on fire. The other purpose was to remove the hot clothes from the pot to the rinse tubs.

After all the things to be washed had gone through the pot to tubs they were ringed by hand to remove all the water that was possible. They were then hung on a clothes line or a wire fence if there was one nearby. This was their home until they were dry.

On the bad days of the winter months they had to be hung anywhere that could be found in the house. But the actual washing always took place outside. Some of the homes had an outside shed or building that was called the wash house. To my knowledge, we ere never fortunate to have a wash house. We always did our laundry outside.

When all the washing was hanging to dry, the water from the iron boiling pot was carried into the house. Mom had a scrubbing brush. She was down on her knees scrubbing the wooden floors with that strong soapy water from the washing.

When she finished the floors were bleached white. Nothing was wasted around our house. That soap did two things. It washed the clothes and the floors in the house.

After the washing was dry, Mom's work wasn't over. She had the ironing to do. This could wait until the next day. Ironing was much more work and a very hot job, especially in the summer time. Mom had four solid flat-irons that would sit on the cook stove in the kitchen or on the hearth in front of the fire in the fire place. She would put her wet finger on the iron to check the temperature After wrapping a cloth around the handle of the iron to keep from getting burned, she would touch the bottom of the iron to check how hot it was. She knew if it was ready by the sound, (hiss) it made when the damp finger touched the bottom of the iron.

Although the women in this mountain area did not have a Lot of education, they had a lot of common sense knowledge and ways of doing the things that had to be done. They knew how to make the starch for ironing by mixing wheat flower with water and how thick to make it.

This ritual went on fifty-two times every year and sometimes more than fifty-two. I never heard my Mom complain about her work. She would sometimes say that she was a little tired. But

Never too tired that she wouldn't cook three meals every day except Sunday. This was the evening we would "snack."

In the late 30s and early 40s there was a washing machine with a roller wringer being sold by Sears and other large companies. The power for operating this machine was a small gasoline engine similar to the ones on the lawn mowers today. It made a lot of noise. This, along with the fumes from the gasoline engine, meant that this modern machine had to be outside when running. Very few people had one of these. Most people didn't have the money to buy one.

I record these accounts of how we lived before all of our push-button things came along. Maybe the generation of today will read this and realize how their forefathers and foremothers did the chores that had to be done.

Uncle Bob

We were living in a section of west Canton that was called Minus Cove. This was on the west side of a mountain called Anderson Mountain. The mountain separated the main road into town, US Route 19, from Stamen Cove. There were log houses all over the east side of this mountain. Several of my mother's aunts and uncles lived on this mountain. The one who was my favorite was Uncle Bob Putnam. He was my Grandma Pressley's brother. She had other brothers and sisters living on the mountain, but Uncle Bob was the one who I remember most.

The people who lived on the mountain didn't come off very often, only when it was necessary — that is, except for Uncle Bob. He did some farming and worked at odd jobs in Canton for the stores that were in town. One of his jobs was with the Parks-Belk department store. This was the largest clothing store in town. He was not a big, fat man, but he was always the Santa Claus at Parks-Belk for about four weeks when the Christmas season came around.

He also was appointed fire warden and game warden. I don't know if either of these jobs had any pay attached to it, but Uncle Bob did a mighty lot of bragging about his titles and his authority. He also was the one person on the mountain who the others looked up to for legal advice. In other words, he was the leader of the Putnam and Pressley clans.

Uncle Bob went to town pretty often, and on the way he would pass our house. He would usually drop in on his way to town, and it was always near dinner (lunch) time. It seemed that everyone had to eat three meals a day along with a snack before going to bed. It didn't make any difference if they didn't have a watch or clock. They always knew when it was time to eat. Uncle Bob knew that our mother would invite him to dinner. I never heard him refuse to eat with us. Dropping by for dinner also gave him a chance to tell us all the news back on the mountain. Most of the news was about whom he caught hunting out of season and who had burned a tobacco bed without asking him before burning. He usually told these people what the laws were, but, as far as I know, he never gave anyone a fine nor has anyone put in jail. He only reminded them he was the law on this mountain.

After finishing eating and letting us know what he had done since the last visit, he would continue his trip to town to visit all his old friends who would always be sitting on park benches trading pocket knives, chewing tobacco, and vying with each other to see which one could tell the biggest tale. For Uncle Bob, this was really living in the fast lane. The simple things made the old folks in the mountains of Western North Carolina happy.

One summer morning, Uncle Bob stopped at our house for his visit and dinner. "Ellen," he said (Ellen was my mother's name), "school is out, and these boys don't have anything to do around here. Why don't you let me take them home with me on my way back this evening?" He was referring to TJ, my brother, and me. "They can help me hoe my corn patch, and I'll take them to the Pigeon River fishing one day."

This seemed like a really exciting invitation to TJ and me. "Moms," we begged, "please let us go. We'll mind everything Uncle Bob tells us."

"All right," Mom said. "But you can only stay one week."

"It's all settled, then," said Uncle Bob. "I'll stop by on my way back from town this evening and take them to my house."

Little did Uncle Bob know what he was getting himself into?

It was about four PM that evening when Uncle Bob came back to our house. "You boys ready to climb the mountain?" he asked. "We'd better get going. It'll be dark pretty soon, and the wild animals 'all be out on the mountain, and I didn't bring my gun."

Things were getting exciting already, and we were not even on our way yet. There were wild animals on the mountain, all right, but Uncle Bob was teasing TJ and me about the danger.

We left for Uncle Bob's house and a full week of fun. We walked on the Minus Cove Road for a ways and then took the foot trail that led to the top of the mountain. It was narrow and rocky, and the farther we went, the steeper it became. This didn't bother uncle Bob because he had made this trip many times and was used to it. TJ and I were not used to such a steep climb; we had been on trails in the mountains a lot, but never on one this steep. Soon we were on the ridge at the top, and the going was easy.

It was nearly dark when we arrived at Uncle Bob's two-room log house. Aunt Roxie, Uncle Bob's wife, was outside in the yard waiting for uncle Bob. She was not expecting any company, and at first she didn't know us. She hadn't seen TJ and me but about twice before. She didn't go anywhere other than to visit the others who lived on the mountain. She seemed happy to have us visit after Uncle Bob told her who we were. We went inside, and Aunt Roxie got a match and lit the coal oil lamp that was on a shelf in the "sitting room." This room was also the cooking and eating room. The other room was only used for sleeping. I never have figured out how they raised seven or eight children in such a small place. All of Aunt Roxie and Uncle Bob's children were grown and had left home by this time. All of them had left the mountain and settled in or near the town of Canton.

It was soon pitch dark and really quiet outside. Every once in a while you could hear an owl, "who…who"; and a couple of times we heard the blood curdling cry of a bobcat. We didn't dare go outside; even though Uncle Bob said it was safe.

"Time to hit the sack," said Uncle Bob, and he went off to the straw tick that was in the corner of the sleeping room. TJ and I were tired from climbing the mountain, and we were sound asleep real soon. Tomorrow wasn't far away with all its promise of the excitement of living in what we called "wild country."

It seemed that we had only been in bed for a short time when we heard Uncle Bob yell, "All right, and boys. Time to get up. Soon be too hot to work in the corn patch."

Up we jumped. We didn't have to dress because we hadn't undressed when we went to bed. We went across the "dog trot" to the cooking-eating-sitting room. Here we saw a big country breakfast that Aunt Roxie had prepared for us.

"You work hands better eat a lot. Long time 'til dinner," said Uncle Bob. He seemed anxious to get to the field and start working on his corn.

We set out toward the field with hoes in our hands.

"Lots of weeds to chop," said Uncle Bob. "Got to get done before it gets too hot to work."

Of course, it never got really hot in the mountains. There was always a cool breeze. It was pretty well known that these mountain men never overworked themselves. They needed a good rest before dinner and a short nap after dinner. There was nothing that was so important that it could not be "put off" until later.

There were about as many tree stumps as there were weeds in that corn patch. We chopped weeds for about two hours, and Uncle Bob said, "We'll take a break now and come back this evening when it gets cooler."

We quit work and headed to the house for our rest before dinner. This was fine with TJ and me. Then, after a good dinner (lunch) and another two-hour rest, we went back to the corn patch to finish chopping the weeds. If we finished the job, we were going fishing the next day, so we also had to dig some worms to use as fish bait. We were pretty busy for the rest of that day. We finished weeding the corn and had a big jar of worms. We were all set for the fishing trip.

We got up at daylight the next day, ate a good breakfast, and went outside to help get the cane fishing poles ready. Aunt Roxie was busy packing a lunch. She was going fishing with us. This was as big a treat for her as it was for TJ and me. She didn't get to go anywhere very often. About the only times she left home was when she went to visit the others who lived on the next ridge or down in the hollow.

When we were all set, off we went down the mountain toward the Stamen Cove Road and on to the "fishing hole" in the Pigeon River.

"How much farther is it?" we asked.

"Oh ... not very far," Uncle Bob said. "We'll be there soon. Another thirty minutes, I guess."

"Do we need a fishing license?" I asked.

"No," said Uncle Bob. "I'm the game warden, and children under twelve don't need one. There won't be any problem. I'm the law."

When we got to the river, we began putting worms on our hooks. Soon, we were all fishing. Aunt Roxie caught the first one: a Horney Head about seven or eight inches long.

"Isn't that a beauty?" she said. And into the sack it went. "Got to get a mess for supper," she said.

It wasn't long until we all had caught a fish. None of them were alike. We had Red Horse, Hog Sucker, Horney Head, and Silversides. We soon had about twenty in the "tow sack" (burlap bag).

"I guess we have enough for supper," said Uncle Bob. "We'd better head out home. I got to scale and gut 'me so Roxie can get 'me on the fire. Better make a new cake of cornbread, too."

We gathered up and headed back toward the mountain and a good meal of fresh fish and corn bread along with a cool glass of fresh churned butter milk. After all this, we were ready for bed and dreams of what we would do tomorrow.

The next morning we were up bright and early as usual. After breakfast Uncle Bob informed us that he would be gone for most of the day. He had "some business" to take care of. He never said what kind of business it was, and we didn't ask him. It must have been something to do with his warden's job.

We loafed around doing some exploring and looking for something to do. Two young boys were not going to sit down and do nothing. Aunt Roxie made a cool drink for us that she called "beer." I don't know what she made it from, but it was very good — nice and cool and sweet. This didn't keep us from becoming bored. We had to find something to do.

Uncle Bob kept a couple of dogs, about ten cats, a cow, some chickens, and a jenny. This jenny would bray with her "hee-haw" so loud that all the people on the mountain could hear her. She, too, didn't work very hard. She only worked when the plowing had to be done or when she was needed to pull a sled to haul corn to the corn mill for grinding. Seems as if everyone and everything took life easy on this mountain.

It wasn't long until we came up with a plan that was sure to create some excitement. The cats were very friendly, and we decided to have some fun with two tom cats that were about half grown. We found some cotton string, and I held the cats in my lap. TJ took their tails and tied them together. There was a wire tied between two trees that Aunt Roxie dried clothes on when she washed. We took the cats that were tied together and put one on each side of the clothes-line wire and let them go. Each cat thought that the other was pulling its tail, so they began to squall and scratch each other. Cat hair was flying everywhere. They made an awful noise. Aunt Roxie came running to get her cats apart and to stop them from killing each other. TJ and I went looking for a hiding place. We laid low for the next few hours.

Uncle Bob came back from his business trip, and Aunt Roxie met him and told what we had done.

"You take those boys back home this minute," she said. "No waiting for tomorrow."

Uncle Bob didn't argue. He knew that she was serious.

We didn't have to do any packing because we didn't bring anything with us. Off we went down the mountain toward Minus Cove and home. This had been a short week. There wasn't as much talking on the way back home as there had been three days earlier. We were soon home, and we didn't stick around to hear what Uncle Bob was telling our mother. We would probably hear from her later. Uncle Bob left for the mountains and his home.

We were never invited to visit our aunt and uncle again. After I returned from overseas after WWII, I went to visit Uncle Bob. This was in 1946. His children had built him a house on the upper end of the Stamen Cove Road and moved him off the mountain. He had an oil heating furnace and a few other things to make living easier for him and Aunt Roxie. He had quit the fire and game warden jobs but was still working as Santa Claus for the clothing store. He didn't mention the cat fight, and neither did I.

My Dog And The Bob Cat

When I was growing up in the 1930s, every young boy had a dog that he could call his dog. This was true with about all the young boys in the mountains of Western North Carolina. It had been this way for over a hundred years, but I don't think that this is the way it is now.

A boy's dog and hunting trips were part of our growing up. We didn't have TV or computer games. We also walked everywhere we went.

A boy having a car was unheard of. If we wanted to go somewhere, we had two choices: either to walk or to ride a horse. I usually chose to walk, especially in the summer. When it was hot, the horse would sweat a lot, and you would have to go to the creek and take a bath after riding because the smell that got on you from the horse was awful.

Back to my dog. My dog was not of any certain breed. If I were to guess, I would say that he was part bulldog (the small breed), and part feisty (the

Rat Terrier type). Most of all, he was my dog. When I was home and had all my chores done, I would take "Spot" (that was his name), and we would go into the woods to hunt. We didn't care what kind of animal we found, whether it be a ground squirrel, a field mouse, a rabbit, or anything, as long as it was small enough so that Spot could handle it. That dog did more barking and digging than he did catching. Anyway, we were hunters, and that was good enough for me and Spot.

There was a family named Lindsey who lived in the same area that we lived in, the Beaverdam Township. I guess the name of the place was chosen long ago because beavers were always damming the creek and causing water to flood the fields nearby. There were two boys in the Lindsey family who were always asking my Dad to take them hunting.

The Lindsey boys had some dogs, but they wouldn't tree a raccoon or a possum. They were rabbit dogs. Dad always kept good hunting dogs. They were always either a blue tick or a redbone breed. His dogs were not allowed to run loose except when they were on a hunting trip.

These dogs were a part of our family, and we always treated them very well. My Dad and the Lindsey boys planned a hunting trip, and I was invited to go along. I was not allowed to bring my dog, Spot. He wanted to run and play a lot, and Dad's dogs were all business. Spot had to stay home.

Most of our hunting was done at night because everyone had to work during the daylight hours. We didn't have any flashlights, only lanterns for light to see our way by and to spot whatever the dogs treed. We filled some lanterns with oil. Dad got his .22 caliber gun ready, and the Lindsey boys had their sling shots and plenty of stones for ammunition. Everyone was excited and ready to get started.

We headed to the watersheds on the mountains at the head of Beaverdam Creek. There was a noise behind us. Dad raised the lantern above his head and there he saw Spot. Spot had made up his mind that he was just as good at hunting as the big dogs, and he was not going to be left out of this "big hunt." We were so far from home that everyone was willing to let my dog come along, but I had to keep him away from the hounds. I agreed to do this.

After about an hour, we were at the foot of the mountain where we were going to hunt for 'coons. We turned the hounds loose, and everyone spoke the familiar words: "Go get 'em, Old' Blue! Go, Red! Go, boy!" Those hounds knew exactly what they were supposed to do.

This was a big night for them, too. They were born to hunt, and they seemed to enjoy it very much.

We kept walking deeper into the mountain forest. Everything was very quiet. We kept going, and every little while Dad or one of the boys would yell out a loud, "Go get 'em, Blue." Soon, we heard one of the dogs begin to let out a long bark every once in a while.

"He's picked up a scent," someone said.

Soon, both dogs were barking, and they were "beginning to sing," according to Dad.

"It won't be long," one of the Lindsey boys said.

Those hounds were going at it hot and heavy. You could tell that they were getting close to their prey. The trail was real hot. We wouldn't have much longer to wait. They would have him "up a tree" soon.

We kept walking as fast as we could toward the sound of the dogs' barking. Then there came what we had been listening for, that "tree" bark. They had something up a tree. We had to hurry to give them some help getting whatever it was out of the tree and on the ground so they could have some fun fighting it.

After what seemed to be forever—climbing up rock cliffs, wading through creeks and spring drains, down on our knees crawling through the thick underbrush, getting scratched from briers—we finally got to the place where the dogs were keeping something up a big tree. Dad put the lantern on his head and began to search the tree.

"There he is. Sittin' in the top, as high as he can get," he said. "You boys see if you can knock him out with your slingshots. I don't want to shoot him unless I have to. The dogs need to have some fun first."

The Lindsey boys got their slingshots out of their overall pockets, each selected a good round rock from their front pockets, and they began to look for eyes shining up in the tree. Every time the critter in the tree looked at the light from the lantern, its eyes would shine like coals of fire.

Flip. Here went a rock. "Missed him," the youngest boy said.

Flip. Flip. More rocks up into the tree. "Got 'I'm," one of the boys yelled. "He's coming' down." They both had hit him.

"Hold the dogs."

"Wonder what it is?"

"Could be a 'coon?"

Down it came. "Bam!" It hit the ground.

"Lord have mercy!" one of the Lindsey boys yelled. "It's a bobcat! And a big un' at that. Turn them dogs loose."

Things were really getting exciting, and the dogs were ready to get that cat. They knew from experience how to "nip" their prey and not let it get hold of them. But this wasn't the way my dog looked at it. The hounds were making more noise than they were biting that cat. Well, my dog had other thoughts about what was going on. I'll show this bunch who really is the brave one around here, he must have thought.

The hounds had the bobcat backed up against a big rock cliff. Here went Old Spot, right between the two hounds and right at that cat. The bobcat jumped up, and Spot ran right under it. The cat landed square on Spot's back, and it sunk its long, sharp claws into him. My dog was trying to get free of the cat, but the cat wouldn't let go.

Off down the mountainside went Spot with that cat riding him like a cowboy rides a horse. The last thing we heard was Spot trying to tell someone to help him get loose from that cat. The hounds had been tied up to keep them from following my dog and the bobcat.

Soon, everything was really quiet—no Spot and no bobcat. We waited for my dog to come back so we could get on with our hunting.

We waited for nearly an hour, and still there was no sign of Spot.

That was over eighty five years ago, and to this day I don't know what happened to Spot. Only that bobcat could tell us what really happened that night.

This is a true account of what went on that night when I went hunting and my dog caught a bobcat.

Saturday Night Bath

When I was growing up in the mountains of Western North Carolina, there was one event that came every week. This was fifty-two times a year and always on a Saturday. And usually the time would be just before we were going to bed for the night. What we did was take our "Saturday night bath." Although we did bathe every day with what we called "wash down as far as possible and up as far as possible," but the whole bath was every Saturday night.

This was not as simple as you may think. There was quite a bit of planning and lots of work in this weekly ritual, and it involved the whole family, that is except for Dad. He usually did his bathing at the paper mill where he worked There were modern bathrooms at the mill complete with a shower room. He took his own soap and towel.

First a large galvanized wash tub was brought into the kitchen. The next thing needed was the water.

Here again it took some manual labor to fill the tub with water for the bath. This usually was the job for TJ, my younger brother, and me. Some places that we lived at had a spring. This meant that there were many trips from the house to the spring with our ten quart water buckets. In our younger days this was quite a task because we were not strong enough to carry a full bucket of water and had to make a lot of trips to the spring.

At other places we lived we usually had a hand dug well with a well box and a windlass with a rope and a water bucket. The bucket was tied to one end of a rope which was wound around the wooden windlass. We would unwind the rope until the water bucket was sunk below the top of the water in the well. Next we would crank the windlass until the bucket with the water was near the top where we could grab-hold and empty it into the tub. We would only fill the tub about half way full. We would fill several large cooking pots and set them on our old wood burning stove. When this water began to boil we poured it in the tub of cold water until it was warm enough to bathe in.

The order of bathing was that the oldest person was always first. The bathing then continued down the line according to age until the youngest was given a bath. Sometimes the water was a bit dirty for the last bather. It depended on how many children there were in the family.

We always used soap for bathing, but sometimes we didn't have "store bought" soap. We then had to use the soap that Mom had made from the excess fat from the hogs that were slaughtered at hog killing. This was a very strong soap that was made from the grease of the fat with lye added. Sometimes the lye had to be made from burning wood and collecting the lye from the ashes. If you were not very careful the soap would make blisters on the skin.

My brother and I sometimes did our bathing in the creek that was close to our home. In the warm summer months this was fine. Not only did we stay clean, but there were some places where the water was deep enough for us to swim. In the cold months of winter we would sometime be brave enough to get in the creek.

A sad note about the creek that we bathed in many years ago: It is now only a trickle of water running down through the fields. I was visiting the community where we lived in the 1930s and saw the sad condition of our favorite bathing place. Only enough water is flowing call it a branch instead of a creek. This is was the year 2007.

My oldest son, Gary, asked me how an adult could bathe in such a small place as the wash tub. I explained that first you would sit in the tub with your legs hanging on the outside. You washed the part of your body that was in the tub then stood up in the tub and finished washing your legs and feet.

This was no problem for us children. We could sit in the tub with our feet inside. We were mountain people and were taught by our elders the way to survive and do the many things that had to be done without any outside help. After all, we didn't have the many things that we have today to make life a lot easier with our daily tasks.

We did survive, we kept our body clean, and we had our "Saturday night bath" in the 1930s.

Neighbors

Back when I was growing up, the word "neighbor" meant more than it does today. Today we refer to the people who live in our neighborhood as our "neighbors," but are they? A very few are real neighbors; the other ones are just people who live close to where you have your house. They never visit or offer to give you a hand when you need someone to help you do a task that you can't do by yourself. They only take care of "number 1" — themselves.

In the community where I grew up, everyone was a real neighbor. You didn't have to ask someone to give you a hand when you needed help. Neighbors were always looking for ways to help someone who needed help. These were true neighbors. Their help was given without any expectations of payment for their services.

Communication was pretty good in the mountains of western North Carolina although we didn't have phones, and very few families had a car. We traveled on foot or by horse and delivered news by word-of-mouth.

We knew when someone died in the community: the bell at the church would toll. We usually knew who had died because we would hear if someone was seriously sick when we went to church services on Sunday. So, when that bell rang at the church, several people would get their mattocks and shovels and head to the church graveyard. We knew there was a grave to be dug. We never thought of asking for pay to dig graves. This was being a neighbor.

I dug or helped dig many graves. They had to be the exact length, width, and depth. The sides were as smooth as glass. Vaults were not used. Digging a grave back then was an art. Not everyone could dig a decent one.

Another example of neighborliness occurred when the Baptists of our community decided that we needed a decent building to hold worship services in. Services had been held in the old one-room school house. A building committee was appointed, and plans were made to begin building a new church building.

The location chosen was near the existing graveyard. On the site was a grove of oak trees that had to be removed before building could begin. My family volunteered to get the trees out of the way. My brother, TJ, and I provided the labor for digging up the tree stumps. We didn't have any dozers or other earth moving equipment in the 1930s. It was all hand work.

We didn't have too much trouble with the smaller trees, but there was a huge red oak that refused to come up. The tap-root was large and grew straight down. We needed help. "Dink" Wines (my well-digging buddy's brother) and my dad came to our rescue. One evening after they came home from work, they placed dynamite under the tree root. We stood at a safe distance, and after a loud boom, our tree was out of the ground.

I did lots of other work building the church like helping dig the basement. We used horses to pull the plows and scoop pans. It was slow, but everyone was patient.

The building started taking shape. Rock and brick masons were hired. A carpenter supervisor was hired to oversee building the church structure. When I later helped the builders, I was paid 10¢ (ten cents) an hour.

Soon the building was completed with a bell tower, a basement, and a beautiful sanctuary for church services. Everyone was proud of this new church. Its name was "Oak Grove Baptist Church." If anyone had seen the spot where the church was built, he would know why this name was chosen.

Within the year, our neighbors who belonged to the other neighborhood church, the Methodist church, decided that they also needed a new church. Their building committee was headed up by Kelley Caswell. He was a very popular person, especially with the young men of the neighborhood. He formed clubs for us and took us fishing and camping at places where we had never been.

The Baptist church was brick. The Methodists decided to build their church with mountain stone. The stone was free for the hauling out of the pastures on the side of little Sam Mountain. Kelley had a large truck that he donated for the rock hauling. He called for volunteers to do the collecting and hauling. He had no trouble getting all the help he needed from both the Methodists and Baptists, and he began hauling rocks from the Mountain. Soon he had a large pile of stone in the field near where the new church was to be built.

Digging the basement wasn't too much of a job. There were no trees to be removed as there were at Oak Grove. Masons and carpenters were hired, and the building was on its way. I worked some on this church, too. I mixed cement for the rock masons, and they paid me the usual ten cents an hour.

This new church would be called "Rockwood Methodist Church." We now had two new churches in our area, but things didn't change in our neighborhood. We were still neighbors. When one of our two churches planned a program, it planned it so that it would not conflict with a program at the other church. The Baptists would attend the Methodist church for their programs, and the Methodists would attend the Baptist church for their programs. Again, we were neighbors.

I have my doubts that anything similar to what we did would ever happen in these so called modern times. In those days, if any of our neighbors was behind in gathering his crops because of sickness or any other unforeseen problem, his neighbors — whether they be Baptist or Methodist, Republican or Democrat, or whatever — always came to his rescue. Wouldn't it be wonderful if things were like that in this day-and-time? We now live closer to each other. We have telephones, newspapers, televisions, cars, and other ways to communicate with each other, but do we these means of communication to get to know the ones who live in our neighborhoods as neighbors? I'm afraid not. We live near each other, but are we really neighbors?

Preacher Bruce

The next and an important part of the family on Mountain Top was the Baptist preacher . He was the pastor of a small church about three miles down the valley in the community. He would have service every Sunday morning and every Wednesday might. The remainder part of his time was used for visiting the ones that couldn't come to church and the ones that wouldn't come.

"Preacher Bruce," as everyone called him would always ride his big bay mare when he made the many trips up and down the hills and hollows visiting . He didn't need an invitation or appointment, finding someone home was all he needed to remind them of all the good things and what would happen with those doing the bad things. If they got a little nervous when he was telling about the bad, this didn't bother "Preacher Bruce."

Preacher Bruce loved to visit everyone but his favorite visit was Ellen, Joe and all ten of their children that lived in that old shackled house on the side of the mountain. Along with the name of the children beginning with the oldest one.

First there was Jim, the oldest at age sixteen. Then Mary just near fifteen. In order was Sally, Bob, Henry, Sarah, Jack, Bill, Lula and Fanny. The mother, Father five boys and five girls made a family of twelve. The last name of the family wasn't important and will not be told to protect the family name.

All the people mentioned on Mountain Top as part of the family will be people that will be the ones most mentioned in the story.

♫ When the roll ♫ is called up— ♫ —

"It's Preacher Bruce — It's Preacher Bruce," all the children on Mountain Top were hollering.

"Don't see him but he always sings while riding 'Old Nell,' that old mare," Sarah hollered.

"There he is, there he is. See — coming up the trail," Bob and Henry pointing to "Old Nell."

All the younger children were running to meet the Preacher.

Preacher Bruce stopped Old Nell and said, "You children step back. Old Nell is old and can't see as well as she use to, wouldn't want her to step on anyone."

He removed the bits from Nell's mouth and said to her, "You can eat on them young saplings and get a good mess while me and the children visit. Won't have to feed you tonight," looking the mare directly in her eyes.

"Saw your dad going up by the spring as I drove up," Preacher Bruce said.

"Does it every time, when he hears you coming he heads for the hills. Been doing this ever since you has a good talking with him," Jim said.

The preacher sat down on the porch and all the children found a seat around him.

"Which do we start first, the songs or the stories?" Preacher Bruce asked.

"Let's sing first," all the girls were hollering.

"We want to hear all them good stories," the boys were protesting.

"Calm down, calm down, we will sing the songs then do the stories" the Preacher said.

" The stories about the young boy who killed the big giant and only used a rock and the swing from his pants." Little Bill said.

"And how that great big fish got hungry and eat Jonah in one big bite, didn't even chew him up, but he jumped out." Henry said.

"Who will start the first song," the preacher asked?

" I will," Mary the oldest girl said.

♪ This little light ♪ of mine, I'm gone ♪ let it shine ♪ — let it ♪ shine—

After singing three songs and telling the stories about the boys heroes they all stood up and walked by the preacher as he was beginning to leave. Preacher Bruce noticed the smile on the mother. He also saw the daddy out close enough where he could hear the stories .

"Come here Nell," he hollered to his mare. "Getting late, got to get home before dark." He kept giving orders.

"Be back to visit as soon as I get time," "Don't forget your prayers every night."

He was on the mare and on his way home —
♪ In the sweet ♪ ♪ ♪ — ♪

By an by ♪ — ♪ ♪ —he could hear him singing as he rode out of sight.

Possum Dinner

The house where we lived in the Thicket section was designed for safety in case the house ever caught fire, It had three bed rooms, a kitchen and what was called a polar or setting room All the rooms had a door between them . The house was built in an "L" shape with a door that opened to the outside where there was a porch the length of the house.

This house was where a prosperous farmer had raised his family. His name was Chad Wallace. Everyone called him "Uncle Chad."

His children were all married and had their own house located somewhere on the Wallis farm. Uncle Chad's wife had died several years ago and he was living with his son. Uncle Chad rented his old homestead along with the barn, apple orchard, chicken house and wood shed. By renting he received a little money and also the house was maintained to keep it from decaying and falling down. We loved to live her better than any other location we had been in the past. The neighbors were real neighbors. Friendly and helpful to each other.

Uncle Chad was a very active person for someone in their seventies. He was lonely living with his son who like a lot of children, were too busy with doing "Their Thing" and had no time for Uncle Chad, an old man.

His new renters did have time for uncle Chad and welcomed his visits. He usually came to our house every day and it would be before dinner time. And of course he was invited to eat with us which he never refused. He had found a home away from home. He became a part of our family during the day time. He had to walk about a mile from his son's house to our house. He took the "Short Cut." Up the high hill, (To small to be called a mountain), down the other side, across the creek and he was ready for a rest in the rocking chair on the porch.

He would always stay around instill dad came home from working in the paper mill.

Uncle Chad had several weaknesses. Two of the greater, (his favorites) was a little drink of moonshine ever so often and always wanting a good "Possum Dinner." I can find the moonshine but since his wife had died he couldn't get anyone to cook the possum.

Dad solved the moonshine problem by placing a jar in the woods where uncle Chad passed when coming to our house.

He would stop on his way home in the evening and take his median, so he said. His son didn't like for uncle Chad to drink.

He asked where you are getting this whiskey, he asked. You will never know, he said with a smile.

Uncle Chad knew that dad, TJ, my brother and I did a lot of possum hunting. He had seen all the hides (skins) we had on the side of the wood shed. We were curing them for shipment to the fur buyer. One of his visits mom, dad and all us children were good possum dinner before I pass on. Getting older every day, can't be many more years.

I will make the sweet taters and biscuits, you men can do the cooking of the possum. I'll go to my mom's for the day but when I come back there had better not be a mess in my kitchen. And all the dishes and pans better are clean.

Everything for the possum dinner was set except the main course. "The Possum." I and the boys will go hunting one night this week. Just any old possum won't do. Got to get a big old white one. They are always fat.

Come Friday we eat supper, did all of the milking and feeding of the animals. Got a "toe-sack," our lantern and the dog and were off to get that fat possum for Uncle Chad's special dinner before he decided to pass on, as he would say.

We were at the foot of Little Sam Mountain in about thirty minutes. All at once we heard old buster, our dog, give a few barks. Won't be long now, dad said. Old buster has already picked up a trail. "Listen at him." Won't be long.

Sure enough old buster settled down with his tree bark. Keep him up there, dad yelled. Come on, better hurry. We were up, there he is, don't look too big, here, TJ, hold the lantern and I'll shake him out. After a couple of shakes the possum was on the ground. I grabbed old buster to keep him from chewing the possum and running his hide. "Sure is a small one," dad said. Better keep him in case we don't catch any more.

I turned old buster loose and away he went. It didn't take him long to find another one. Better hurry dad said not many out this early so we better get him and get back home. I got to work tomorrow and need to get to bed early. This one was in a bigger tree and up pretty high. Here, hold the lantern as he handed it to TJ. I held the dog and dad began climbing the tree. He was about half way up the tree and he began shaking the top limbs where the possum was setting. All at once he let go of his hold on the limb and down he came. WOW, I hollowed. Sure is a big one, and as white as my hair. Hurry down and put him in the sack before he goes back up that tree.

Dad was down from the tree; the possum was in the sack old buster was tied so he wouldn't take off and tree another one. We had been gone a little over two hours. We headed back to our house.

After we arrived home there were still things to be done. We had to fix a chicken coop to keep the possums in. We would skin the small one the next day and begin feeding the big one all the buttermilk he could eat. Dad wanted him as fast as we could get him.

Uncle Chad came every day to look at what would soon be his big moment. "The Possum Dinner." Dad told him that he would cook that possum on the next Saturday. He was off from work from Friday until Monday morning.

Mom cooked the sweet potatoes on Friday. Made the biscuits the next morning before leaving for Grand Pa Presley's house. Dad had the possum skinned and dressed when uncle Chad arrived. This was the earliest he had ever come to our house. He was as excited as TJ and I was.

We were looking forward to eating our first possum. According to Dad and uncle Chad they had eat possum many of times. One of the best meats," said uncle Chad."

Mom's big canning pot filled with water was on the wood stove and was soon boiling. In went the meat. He was in one piece. We'll pare boil him for about an hour. When he is tender we will put salt and all the other good stuff on him, laid him in this big baking pan and into the oven for a while. Want him done to the bone.

Uncle Chad wouldn't leave the kitchen although it was really warm from the fire in the cook stove even with the windows and door open. He was going to miss anything. Let's set on the porch while it's cooking, Dad said. I think I'll stay here in the kitchen. Man does that smell good.

About an hour later dad went to the stove, opened the oven, and punched a fork in the side of the then brown possum. Ready to take out, he said. Better set the table, are you boys going to eat with us, he asked? Sure are, I said. Never eat any possum before.

Soon the possum, sweet potatoes and biscuits were on the table. One of you boys goes get a jar of buttermilk from the well house. Need something to wash this down.

Uncle Chad and dad wasted no time filling their plate with food. Especially with meat. They began eating like they were starved. I think the two of them slipped around and had a good drink of moonshine. Sort of an appetizer. TJ and I took a little piece of the possum, sweet potatoes and a biscuit. TJ was eating his as though he liked it. I kept chewing the piece I had in my mouth. I couldn't swallow it. It seemed to get bigger and bigger in my mouth. I left the table, went out on the porch where old buster was laying, took that big bite of possum out of my mouth and gave it to buster. He wasted Time in swallowing it, looked at me, wagging his tail begging for more..

Uncle Chad, dad and TJ had finished eating and were cleaning up the table. You boys can help wash these dishes — got to get this place cleaned before your mom comes home,

Everyone except Uncle Chad was washing and cleaning as fast as we could. Soon we were through. Just in time because here comes mom and the two girls, Louise and Levite. My younger sisters. They had taken sides with mom about the cooking of possum in her kitchen.

When they walked in the kitchen they began gathering pots and pans. They found a scrubbing brush, some lye soap and headed toward the creek that run through the pasture behind the barn, Going to scrub these pans with sand. Don't want any of that possum grease in my cooking. Out the door and toward the creek they went. It was getting late in the evening and everything was sort of back to normal. Uncle Chad had left for home, the pots and pans put in their right places in the kitchen. We were all on

The porch when dad spoke. You and the girls sure missed a good dinner. Everything was really good, even if I did cook it. No one answered him. He smiled a little, took out his pipe, put new tobacco in it and struck a match to light the tobacco.

This was many years ago. I don't recall when Uncle Cad died but he did get his last wish before parting this earth.

His little drink every now and then, and the most important thing, the "Possum Dinner."

July 4th
April 1, 1922 – July 4, 2015

Growing up in the years of the Great Depression was not easy. I, like all other boys learned at a very early stage how to take care of ourselves. We knew to work hard and to make do with whatever we had. At the age of 16 I began my first job other than farm work. I made 35 cents per hour working for a program started by President Roosevelt, the National Youth Administration. Next, I enlisted in the Civilian Conservation Corps and went to work in the Great Smokey Mountains at Smokemont, North Carolina. I was working there when World War 2 broke out. I was drafted in the army, reported for basic training, and was sent to Fort Bragg, North Carolina.

We had a welcoming committee: a couple of tough looking sergeants and two corporals. After a cool welcome, we were lined up and marched to the Post barbershop. The barbers would ask how you would like your hair to be cut. But regardless of what you told them, they gave everyone the same style – clipped down to the skin. You weren't in the chair more than two minutes.

Next, we marched to the Supply Room. We got underwear, sheets, blankets, socks, handkerchiefs, a razor, shaving soap, a shaving brush, a toothbrush, toothpaste, hand soap, washcloths, towels, a helmet, a rifle, a web belt, a first aid kit, a gas mask, boots (that were too large), and a duffel bag. We were issued two of almost everything. I had never had this many worldly goods in my whole life. I felt sort of proud to have all of them. But I could barely carry such a load.

The next three months were hectic. We went through KP, guard duty, forced marches, the obstacle course, the rifle range, aircraft shooting, bayonet drill, hand-to-hand combat, and lots of other things to make sure we stayed busy. Then it was time to move out and make room for the next group of soon-to-be soldiers.

They shipped us in different directions. I ended up at Fort Dix in New Jersey. I was assigned as a Supply Clerk with the 90th General Hospital. I was at Fort Dix for about six months before leaving for an overseas assignment. We packed up and boarded a train for New York City and the boat docks. In time we boarded the Queen Elizabeth, the English tourist ship. Back then it was the largest such ship in the world. Over 15,000 troops were on onboard. We crossed the Atlantic by way of Iceland where German submarines couldn't travel because of the ice. The ship sort of zigzagged its course.

We started at Malvern Hills, England for about two months, and then we went again to a town in Wales. We were in Wales for only three weeks. Toward the end of our stay, we began to downsize, getting rid of everything we could do without.

A few days after D-Day we were awakened near midnight, loaded into trucks, and taken straight to the docks where ships were waiting for us. We were loaded onto ships until there was standing room only. We were finally on our way. The English Channel was very rough that morning. The ship was a small one and was rising and falling with every wave. An announcement came over the ship intercom telling us that we were on our way to France. The Germans had been pushed back, and we would land at Omaha Beach.

It was near daylight and you could see the outline of land in the far-off distance. We went in as far as the ship could go. Then we had to climb down rope webs to the landing craft that were waiting below. They were small: each would carry about fifty soldiers with their equipment. They were bobbing up and down more than the ship.

The landing craft rammed into the sand quite a ways from land. We had gone in at low tide. The front end of the boat was a big gate. It was let down until the end of the landing craft was wide open, and we hit the water. The surf was deep enough to be above our waist. There was nothing to do but keep moving toward dry land. We were lucky: The Germans had been pushed back to St. Lo, and we didn't have to dodge bullets. We only had the cold water and the debris floating around everywhere to put up with. On the beach, the ground was covered with abandoned and damaged equipment, both German and American

We finally got together as a group and started inland. We stopped in a field at Charente about five miles from St. Lowe where General Patton's Third Army was trying to take the town. We were not assigned to any outfit at this time. We budded up with someone, and between the two of us we pitched a pup tent. We were given "K rations" for our meals. Some of the meals were OK. You never knew what was in the package until you opened it. The cheese, eggs, potted ham, and beans were all right. I never liked the stew — it was too greasy to eat cold. Sometimes this was better than going hungry.

The next morning when I was looking around, I saw a very large field that was turned into a graveyard. It was estimated that there were twenty thousand solders buried there. There were white crosses as far as you could see. Also, there were huge piles of shoes and clothing nearby. I'm sure these belonged to those who were buried there. I found a pair of trooper boots my size, took off my old stiff boots, threw them into the pile, and put on the softer boots. I wore these for the next year or so.

My unassigned status didn't last long. On the third day I was assigned to a twenty-five man crew who were to drive in the "Red Ball Express." These were vehicles carrying supplies to the front lines. We didn't know what we were hauling. There was only room for one person, a driver, in each vehicle.

I was on this assignment until we reached Metz, France. I then was assigned to a Military Police unit. Our duty was to take prisoners back to stockades in France. One cold winter day I had about fifteen prisoners holding them for a pick up crew to come and get them and take them to a stockade farther south. The day went by, and no one came to get the prisoners until nearly dark that evening. I became so cold I was numb, and my feet were frost-bitten. I came down with pneumonia and was put in the hospital at Verdun. I was given penicillin shots every four hours for two days and then sent back to my unit.

I was assigned as a guard to a stockade near a little town named Bar le Duck. Things were going pretty well until the Germans made their last counter-attack, known as the "Battle of the Bulge." Everyone who could be spared was sent to the "Bulge." I was put on duty at the stockade twenty-four hours a day. The weather was miserable, with snow, fog, and cold, so air support couldn't help. These conditions lasted for over a week, and then the sun came out. There were clear skies, and the Allied air attack began. The sky was black with airplanes — bombers, fighters, and everything. They flew continuously all day long. The Germans were pushed back, killed, or captured.

The war was near an end in Europe, and it wasn't long afterwards that the Germans gave up and called it quits. We began to let the prisoners go back home. I was ready to go home too.

Those going back to the United States were prioritized based on how many dependents we had, how long we had been in service, how long we had been overseas, and other factors. My priority points put me in about the middle of the list.

My group was loaded on a train and sent to a port in Belgium. We stayed there another six to eight weeks, and then we boarded a "Liberty Ship." It had been over twenty-eight months since I had any milk. I volunteered for KP duty on the ship so I could have all the milk I wanted. I think I drank ten pint cartons on my first day at KP.

We docked in New York, and from there we were sent to a camp in Virginia then back to Fort Bragg, the same place I had started from about four years ago. There I was to be processed for separation from the Army. Finally, I was a civilian again and was on my way home.

My service in WWII was an experience that I will never forget. There were all types of people in this war. Each person was assigned to a certain job and they did what they were told to do. Never did I hear anyone say, "I don't want to do this, let someone else do it." Many were praised as heroes and were awarded medals. I received medals and ribbons. Many others were never mentioned or received any medal. But my way of thinking, all that served in this war were heroes. True, some captured many enemies, some none. But without everyone the war would have been lost. We all had a job and we did our part.

Today we celebrate the 4th of July as a day for picnics, swimming and dozens of other events. Stop for a moment and think of the real reason that July 4th is a holiday.

English Vacation

The names used are the inventions of the author who apologizes should I have inadvertently used the name of any actual person.

On December 1943 I left New York City, USA on the Queen Elizabeth luxury liner along with twenty thousand other soldiers on a cruise across the Atlantic ocean by the route of Iceland on my way to England . Eleven days later we were in The Firth of Clyde.

My next ride was on a rail train much different from what we road on in the USA. I enjoyed the seating in the small compartments .

My first stop in England was near a town that had walls all around the city. We were only there for a few days but I did visit a very large castle on a large hill. The Nuns from the churches were using it to care for the children that were misplaced from the war.

My next short stay was in a larger town named Manchester. I enjoyed my stay here and meet several pretty English girls. Never tried to remember their names. Although it was sad with the bombing of England There was time for a little fun time. This usually was a dance that I would join in without an invitation. No big band, a Accordion and a drummer. We enjoyed each other's company and had fun.

Next stop, A city of newel built buildings in large farm fields called Malvern. This would be my home for a few months. We were moved around quite often. This would keep the Germans always on alert as to when we would be invading them.

One thing I did not like was the Italian POW's that worked on the farms getting the attention of the pretty young ladies that lived on the farms with them. Although they were not allowed off the farms they still got the girls attentions.

Not far from Malvern was a small city that had everything we soldiers needed for our vacation away from home. Plenty of pretty girls, Theaters, Pubs and more Pubs. A beautiful river for taking a walk along with your girl friends. And a large hotel that the American Red Cross operated where we could spend the night in town. This was the city called WORCHESTER.

We as strangers from another country, fun loving, and more money to buy whatever we wanted were welcomed to their country. We had as much fun as they did while playing darts and drinking warm beer as the locals Pub. My favorite Pub was located at the fork in a small road about half way between Malvern and Worchester.

When visiting the Pub I usually brought along a couple of Prince Albert or Half And Half tobacco for my old English friends who smoked their pipes. They called them their Pips. Usually the warm beer drinks were free for me. No Pub was without a dart board and I was always challenged for a game. The old timers would shut one eye, and throw the dart that usually hit the center bull eye. When it was my turn I usually missed the complete board but received a standing ovation complete with hand claps. We were from different countries but we were friends that I never forgot as I moved on in my journey.

In my five month stay in England I was in the cinema only once and this was not a planned visit. I always preferred the dances although they were quite different from the ones we did in the USA. But they were fun. I never learned the name of the dance but they went something like this. You put your left foot in- put your left foot out-do the hokey pokey and turn all about- that's what it's all about. (Something like this?). Back to the cinema.

When I arrived to Malvern I was assigned to the 90th. General Hospital supply duty. Sort of double duty for me because I could carry a gun that the Hospital Doctors, Nueces and Orderlies could not carry. This was their guard security. One of my duties while in supply was my going along with the trucks that brought the laundry to the Court Steam Laundry in Birmingham. I did the paper work for getting the laundry in and the cleaned laundry back every week. The laundry was very large and I would guess that there were fifty or more employees working there. The part I liked most was that most of the workers were girls. There were girls of all ages, all sizes, and pretty ones ugly ones all there for the same reason. Do their part to help with this awful war. Of course the girls were interested in we GI's as much as I was in them. I spotted a cute little read-head girl and interdicted myself. In nothing flat I had a date for Saturday in Worchester. It so happened that the little read-head was the daughter of the laundry owner and had a large home in Worchester where they stayed on the weekends. I had a date for the coming Saturday to meet in town and another date on Sunday for lunch and meeting the family. This was my lucky day.

It so happened that Saturday was my twenty second birthday and I invited one of my friends to come along to celebrate the event. We had our passes for the week end, checked out bicycles from the supply and on our way to Worchester. It was near noon time when we arrived in town and decided to find a good bar and do a little "birthday celebrating." Little did James an I would celebrate to much with scotch and gin instead of the warm beer. By late evening we both had drank to much. We were drunk.

"I have to go and find that pretty little Red Headed girl that was to meet me this evening. I never found her she found me. With her help she had me in the balcony of the local cinema. Where I went to sleep.

When she woke me up the movie was over. I was ashamed of myself for what I did on my first date . She told me her name was Pat and that I was to meet her family the next day. With her help I found the hotel that the American Red Cross operated for soldiers.

Early the next morning I was awoken by someone that there was someone at the hotel door asking for me. I had not undressed from the night before so I went to the hotel door. There was Pat, the little read headed girl that had rescued me from the MP'S the night before.

"Get dressed, my family are waiting for you at our house. They want to meet you before lunch time.." Pat said to me. I went back inside, washed up, put my tie on but couldn't find my cap.. Pat noticed that my cap was missing. I told her that it was lost. She took me to the cinema, we went up to the balcony too where I was the night before and there was my hat lying on the floor.

I met Pat's family. Her mother, dad, and her younger sister. After a very nice lunch that I didn't eat very much of the father invited me to his literary, offered me a cigar and ask me to have a seat. He asked me about my family back in the US, my plans after the war, and if I knew how he could invest money in my home town. All my answers were negative. My head was aching and I wanted to get out other as soon as I could. Pat again came to my rescue. She knocked on the door and asked me to come down so they could take a walk before I had to return to Malvern. I returned back to camp and my duties including my visits to the laundry in

Birmingham. I avoided Pat as much as I could and never had a date with her.

On one of my visits to the laundry I bumped into a very pretty girl. She was taller than Pat, had long wavy hair and gave me a big smile. I put my arm around her shoulder and asked her where her home was.

She was from a section called Small Heath. I invited her to take the train to Worchester on a Sunday and we would go somewhere for a picnic lunch. The date was made. Next Sunday on the early train from Birmingham to Worchester. My name is Brenda, Brenda Bayless she told me.

On Sunday I was up at day break, went to the mess hall and asked my friend the mess officer to make me box of sandwiches for me to take my girl friend on a picnic. I eat a hasty breakfast , checked out a bicycle and was on my way to Worchester with my box of sandwiches. I arrived before the train from Birmingham arrived and anxiously waiting for my new girl friend. The wait was short. There came the train and Brenda was one of the first to get off. I welcomed her with a big hug and asked where she would like to go. She said that this was her first visit to Worchester. In fact her first visit anywhere outside of Birmingham. I saw a nice place down near a river when I come into town. I told her.

"Any place is fine with me," she said.

We found a nice grassy place to set near the river, talked a lot while holding hands, she never forced herself for love on me or did I toward her. We were both well mannered to each other. Time went fast and it was time to get back to the train station. With a short kiss we left promising to speak on my next time to the laundry where she worked. We did talk the next day I was in Birmingham. I informed her that I would not see he again as I was moving to somewhere but did not know where. We promised to keep in touch by mail. She gave me her mailing address and I gave her my APO mailing address. Don't know why but I there was something different between Brenda and me than it was with other girls I met in England. I promised to come visit her when I could With a short kiss I never saw Brenda again.

Fox Hunting

In the mountains of Western North Carolina it was natural that the oldest son would learn about guns and know how to hunt when he was the age of ten to twelve. His knowing how to hunt would help supply the meat for the family table. I was one of those boys.

I was around eleven when I first started hunting squirrels, rabbits and pheasants and heard of fox hunting but had never been on one.

One day I heard dad talking with two of his friends about going fox hunting. His friends, Dave and Joe always kept dogs that were called fox hounds. I asked if I could go along on this hunt with them.

"Sure, be glad to teach you if Fletch will let you go" Dave said.

It was all set. The fox hunt would be this coming Saturday night and I was invited.

About five o'clock on Saturday evening I was in the A-Model headed to Dave's house. Joe was already there when we arrived. There were three dogs in the truck seat of Dave's truck. Sally, Nell and old red was their names and they belonged to Dave.

Each hunter, except me began to load the sack they had brought along. We were soon on our way up the road to Beaverdam Mountain. Dad in the a-model, Dave and Joe in the truck.

We went up an old logging road as far as they could with the cars and parked. Dave was leading his dogs, Joe and dad carrying the sacks. I was having a pretty big job just keeping up with the hunters.

Finally we arrived to a flat field at the top of the mountain. I could see that there had been others there from the big circle of rocks that was used for the fire. Also someone had left a big pile of wood for us to burn.

Dave turned the dog's aloes and the sacks with whatever they had brought was set by the circle where the fire would be.

"Where are our guns?" I asked the hunters?

"Guns, that's a bad word. If someone should kill a fox they would "Blackballed" the rest of their life." I decided not to ask any more questions, just watch, I said to myself.

Joe was back from the spring on the mountain side with a sock lard bucket full of water. He put it on the fire that was burning in the circle, took some coffee out of the sack and dumped it in the water. This would be the coffee for the night.

Everyone had claimed their favorite place to set around the circle where the fire was burning. Dave raised his head up with his hand around his ear.

"Listen he said there goes Sally, and old red is joining in. WHOOP-EE, GO GET EM," Dave said.

"Ain't that the prettiest music you ever heard, SING TO HIM," Joe hollered.

"I'm a little thirsty," Dad said.

"Out of the sack came a half gallon fruit jar. I was thinking this was water for us to drink but after Dave, Joe and dad passed it around they didn't offer a drink. It didn't take me long to figure it out what they were drinking. I could smell it all the way across the fire.

All three of the dogs were barking as loud as they could and the hunters were hollering about what pretty music that was. To me it only meant that three dogs were trying to catch what I guessed was a fox.

I went in the trees close by and gathered me some cedar limbs and made me a bed on the back side of the fire. I was getting sleepy. I was soon asleep.

It was getting day light when I woke up. I looked around and there was the three fox hunters sound asleep. Lying by was the half gallon water jar, "Empty." All three of the dogs had found them a bed and were sound asleep.

Everyone was soon awake, dogs loaded in the truck, sacks loaded and we were down the mountain headed back home.

This was my first fox hunt. And my last trip listing for some dogs run just to hear them barking.

It was fall season here in the mountains. All the but bearing trees were loaded with nuts for the animals that lived in these mountains. To me it meant "Squirrel hunting time." I was nearly twelve years old and ready to go.

I was out of bed while mom was cooking breakfast for the family. She had started the cooking especially for me because I was going squirrel hunting. This was the first hunt this season. I had me a place staked out on Clark Mountain. There was a large grove of hickory trees and they were loaded with nuts. I would have to fight them off I told my mom.

The five thirty morning whistle at the paper mill was the squirrels started feeding, blowing when I was leaving the house headed to the cove on Clark Mountain. I had been this trip many times before and knew exactly where the trails were. I wanted to be there before

I found my way a good place on the side of the ridge where I could see all over the hickory trees.

It was nearly day light. I was setting very quite when I heard something moving in the leaved down the hollow where I was setting. I strained my eyes and finally located what was making the leaves move around. There walking up the trail leading to where I was setting was an animal I had never seen. Or at least I didn't recognize it.

A few days early there was talk of seeing a panther in our part of the mountain. I began to picture all kind of wild animals coming straight to where I was setting.

I pulled the hammer back on my twelve gauge shoot gun, raised it to my shoulder and sighted it straight to whatever was coming to get me. I had decided that I wouldn't let him get too close to me. The more I looked the bigger that thing got. I decided that this was long enough. I took a good sight, pulled the trigger, "BANG." There was a blood curdling scream, flopping and kicking and then everything became quite.

I put another bullet in my old shot gun, goy up and started walking very slowly down the trail to see what I had shot. I took my foot and turned whatever it was over. There it was. The largest gray fox I had ever seen. I kicked him a few more times to see if he was dead.

With the goon shot and I moving around all the squirrels were gone. I asked myself. What can I do with this beautiful animal?

"I'll take it home ". I said.

I took some small rope from the pocket of my duck back hunting coat I always wore when hunting. I tied the fox feet together, hung him on my shoulder and headed for home.

I stopped at the wood shed and lade the fox down and hollered for my mom to come out. She comes to where I was trading by the fox.

"Look what I killed" I showed her.

"Guess I'll skin it and send it along with the possum hides I have," I said to mom.

"Better not let these fox hunters know you killed a fox, no telling what they would do to you," my mom said.

No one ever found out that I had killed a fox. I skinned it and shipped it along with the other hides I had nailed on the side of the wood shed.

This was a "Real Fox."

WAL-MART COWBOY

Wal-Mart is my favorite store and this is where I do most of my shopping. I like Wal-Mart for several reasons. Their associates are friendly and helpful. The variety, choices of brand name products, freshness of food and all the other things that make them a "One-stop Store."

They also consider their customers needs, One being their health and how to assist them on getting around in this very large store. Making it easy for them to find the items they are looking for.

Every visit to Wal-Mart I see men and women doing their shopping the easy way. Going from aisle to aisle in the battery powered "Shopping Carts." I also notice that some of them don't have a lot of anything in their baskets. And at times if I really noticed what they had in the basket the last time I saw them they had exchanged it for something different. Just the same, they were doing some, "Big Shopping."

Now that I am 93 years old and my legs along with other parts of my body seem to tire a lot easier I have been giving some consideration to join the regulars on the race track at "Wal-Mart'.

Today while at the store convinced me that I was eligible for one of these motorized shopping carts.

Why did I decide today?

I was in the pharmacy area when I spotted a driver that I had never seen before. I usually don't pay very much attention to the "Demolition Derby" but what I saw today was something that I am sure others shoppers noticed.

Here was a young feller, (probably early 40s), He was dressed for the occasion Ten gallon cowboy hat, cowboy boots, western jeans complete with a leather belt and silver buckle. He could have been a stand-in for most any of the cowboys I watched at the movies on Saturday seventy / eighty years ago.

As I made my way around the store locating what I needed I saw this "Cowboy" several timed. I became sort of nosey and began to look to see what he was buying. When I first saw him in the pharmacy area he didn't have anything in the basket. All I noticed was the big grin on his face; He was enjoying his Saturday drive.

The next time he passed me he had a gallon of milk in the basket. An isle or two later he must have changed his mind. He didn't need the milk. He needed what looked like a "throw rug." When I saw him next.

I found what I came for so I pushed my buggy toward the check-out station. And this was when I saw the "Cowboy" for the last time. What did he have in his basket? It sure wasn't the throw rug. But I did see one of the happiest customers at "Wal-Mart Super Store."

I have given some serious thought of trading the buggy I push and use to steady myself for one of the electric buggies and join the "Cowboy "on Saturdays.

I'll do my buying at Wal-Mart on another day. May talk the "Cowboy" into a race down the main aisle.

Trading Cows

I guess it is also the nature of man to barter and trade with someone with the intention of getting the better of the deal. This was true of my dad. He would trade anything he had always thinking that he was getting the better part of the deal.

There was one such deal that he did when I was about ten years old that I will never forget. It was a deal that involved our only source of milk and butter. This was our big jersey cow that gave our family nearly ten quarts of rich milk twice every day. Once each morning and again that evening my brother TJ did the milking, and there was so much milk that he couldn't carry it to the house. TJ was only nine years old. Mom had to go to the barn and bring the milk to the house.

We never had the faintest idea that this member of our family would be involved in one of Dad's "swapping deals." But our cow was about to move to a new home. It happened at a time when Mom was visiting her mom and dad. She was gone for only one day, but the setting was perfect for one of the biggest and worst trades that Dad ever made.

A drinking buddy of Dad's came to visit the day that Mom was away visiting. His name was Jack Blankenship. He lived in the old Sam Robinson home place off the Thickety Road. It was a short ways from the Oak Grove Baptist Church. We were living in an area known as "Hainty Hollow." Lots of people stayed away from this area at night. They were superstitious and believed all the scary things that they had heard about ghosts that were in the near by graveyard. We lived there for several years and never saw any ghosts, but we children would not go near the graveyard after dark.

Well Jack and Dad were standing at a big spring that was at the foot of a big maple tree. We had a spring box there where Mom kept her milk and butter in the cool water that was flowing from the spring. The refrigerator was not a common thing in the home at this time (the 1930s) where we lived. The spring box was also where Dad usually kept a half gallon fruit jar of homemade moonshine, (corn liquor). It was where he entertained his friends when they came to visit. I think this was the reason that he had a good bit of visitors. They enjoyed the cool spring water that they used to get the sting from their throat caused by the "white lightning." Here was the perfect time and place for Jack to get him a good cow and get rid of the one he had that was going dry.

Now our cow had come to the drain from the spring for a drink of water.

"Say, Fletch? How would you trade that cow of yours for a real good cow that will have a calf pretty soon? You could probably get four or five dollars for the calf if it's a heifer. If it's a bull calf you can feed it real good for about six months and kill it for veal. Probably get a hundred cans from it."

He wasn't as far along with the drinking as Dad was, so he was taking advantage of this to make a trade.

"Well, my cow won't have a calf for quite some time, and I could use an extra five dollars. I'll trade with you. I'll get one of the boys to go home with you and bring your cow back."

The deal was made and, I went with Jack and brought back the new cow. Mom came home a little before dark, and one of the first things she saw was the strange animal.

"That's our cow," TJ said. "Dad and Jack Blankenship traded cows today. Don't know why though. Our old cow gave plenty of milk and it was pretty rich. Had about two inches of cream on a bucketful. Dad just likes to do some trading, I guess."

She told Dad, "You take that cow back this very minute and bring my cow home."

"I can't go tonight. I'll talk to Jack tomorrow."

"You'd better," Mom said. "TJ, you'd better go and milk her if we have to wait until tomorrow to take her back to Jack."

TJ got a big two and a half gallon bucket and headed to the barn. He wasn't gone long until he came back to the house with the milk. He didn't have to have Mom come carry the milk to the house because he had milked only about one gallon from this cow. It was nothing like the big bucket of milk from our cow that Dad had traded.

Mom began to cry. "We won't have enough milk, and I can't give the Holland family any. Their little children will be without milk because they don't own a cow. And this milk is so skimpy that I won't have any cream to churn to make butter for the table. How could anyone be stupid enough to trade a good cow for one that is skin and bones and doesn't give enough milk for our family?"

Dad hung his head down, and out the door he went. I followed him and said, "You'd better think of some way to get our cow back, or you'll never see any peace of mind around here."

"I know," he said. "The first thing tomorrow morning you make a trip to Jack's house. When no one is around, you tell him that I have some mighty fine peach brandy, and if he would come over, I'll let him sample it. This will get him to come, and I'll think of someway to get our cow back."

Sure enough, Jack was at our house around dinner time. His twelve year old son, Willard, came, too, so he could visit with TJ and me. Mom invited them to eat with us, but they said they were not hungry. Dad rushed through his meal and headed to the spring box and to the moonshine that he had added peach flavoring to. Jack was right behind him, and it was not long until they were sampling the "peach brandy."

After about an hour and a dozen samples of the brandy, Dad and Jack were doing a lot of talking. Dad had made it a point to not drink very much but gave Jack all he wanted.

"Say, Jack," Dad began. How would you trade me my cow back? The old woman is having a fit over me letting you have her."

"I don't know," Jack said with a slur in his speech. "My old woman likes that cow. Haven't had this much milk from any cow that I've owned before."

Dad saw right away that Jack wasn't about to part with his new cow without some kind of a barging.

"Tell you what I'll do," Dad said. "I'll give you your cow back and throw in one of them OIC pigs out in the hog lot."

"I don't know," Jack said. "I guess I could use a hog for our winter meat. We don't have one. I don't want to part with this good cow, but seeing as to the trouble you are in with your old woman, I'll trade with you."

"Go get a sack," Dad told TJ. Need something to carry the pig over to Jack's house. Put a halter on the cow. You and Charles can go with Jack and Willard and bring our cow back."

Off we went, Willard with the pig in the sack thrown over his shoulder and TJ leading the cow. Jack was staggering along behind. That peach brandy was working on old Jack.

It was during the summer months, and it was pretty warm. We had traveled to "Home Brew Knob," about half way, , when Jack said, "I need to stop and rest."

Willard took the sack with the pig in it off his shoulder and laid it on the ground. "This pig has finally quit kicking. Must've gone to sleep."

Willard opened the sack to take a peak. "Dad, I believe the pig is dead," said Willard."

"No, son. He's not dead; he's resting. Close that sack and let's get on home."

When we reached Jack's house, Willard set the sack with the pig in it on the ground. "Dad, I believe this pig is really dead."

"If he's dead, you're the one who killed him. Take him to the pig pen and let him go. He'll be OK."

Willard emptied the sack, but the pig didn't move. He hollered to his Dad, "This pig is dead! What do you want me to do with him?"

"Willard, you killed my pig," he said to his son. "We can't waste that good meat. Bring him to the house. I'll dress him, and we will eat him for supper."

TJ and I put the halter on our old cow and started to make our way back home. TJ said, "I bet Dad won't ever trade off our cow again."

Anyhow, everyone was happy. Mom had her cow back, and Jack and his family made the best supper that they'd had in a long time out of that dead pig.

Model 'A' Ford

I was sixteen years old now and had a good job. I was working for the National Youth Administration (NYA). This was another program of President Roosevelt's New Deal. The purpose of the program was to give young men a chance to learn a trade and at the same time earn some money.

Our work included many projects. We cleaned off graveyards that had been neglected for many years. We built football fields complete with stadiums. They were made of mountain stone. Some are being used today. There was plenty of stone on the mountainsides, so material didn't cost anything.

The largest project I worked on was a garage for state-owned school buses. It was located in Waynesville and was also made from stone. All the work was supervised by qualified stone masons. Our work schedule was two weeks of work at 40 hours a week and two weeks off. The pay was thirty cents an hour. This was the highest pay I had ever received.

The job in Waynesville created a problem for me. It was over twelve miles away from where I was living. It was impossible for me to walk that distance and be on time to go to work, so someone from our area had to buy a car. I was in town one Saturday (as I was every Saturday). I went to Mr. King's used car lot. Mr. King was the husband of my former school teacher at Beaverdam. I was looking around the car lot, and Mr. King came out and asked if he could help me.

"I'm looking for a car," I said. "What is the cheapest one you have?"

He pointed to a Ford Model A touring car. It was black with no curtains and bad tires, but it had a good cloth top, the paint was good, and there weren't any dents or scratch marks on it. To me it was a beauty.

"How much?" I asked.

"Sixty dollars," he said.

"Sure a lot of money," I said. "I'll think it over. I may come back after a while."

After the usual Saturday movie—a western and a Popeye Cartoon—I went back to the car lot to see if the Ford was still there.

It was. So was Mr. King.

"I can't get that much money today," I told Mr. King.

He looked me over pretty well and said, "I know money is scarce, and young men your age don't get very much work. I'll tell you what I'll do. If you can get forty-five dollars today, I'll let you have the car for that much."

I already had thirty dollars from my NYA pay, so off I went looking for fifteen dollars. I found my brother, TJ, and told him I needed forty five dollars, and I had only thirty. I told him if he would lend me fifteen dollars, I could buy a car, and I'd pay him back when I got my next pay, and I'd teach him how to drive. He told me he'd let me have the loan.

Whoopee! My problem was solved.

I went back to the car lot and bought the car. By the time Mr. King had made out the bill of sale and had put enough gas in the tank to get me home, it was well after dark. I was afraid to drive through town although there wasn't any traffic. The road home was paved to the edge of town at the Fiberville Bridge. I started looking for someone to drive the car to the bridge for me. I found my friend Bill Cordell, my partner on the air plane ride. I explained my problem to him, and he said he would help me. He drove the car to the Fiberville Bridge.

Off we went around the Pigeon River Road. Only about three miles, and I would be home to show off my prize possession. It took me quite a while to make those three miles. Steering the car was hard for me. Cars didn't have any power steering back then. They only had mechanical steering. You had to turn the steering wheel nearly all the way around before it would turn the front wheels.

I finally arrived at the cattle gate that was across the road that led to our house. The road was on the side of a steep hill and only wide enough for one car to travel it. Well, I chickened out. I was afraid to try to drive on that narrow road, and I wasn't about to leave my car sitting on the main road.

It was about one A.M. by then. Everyone was in bed asleep. I had no choice but to walk to the house and get my dad to drive the car to the house. I woke him and explained the problem. He got out of bed, put on his clothes, and went to get the car. The commotion had everyone awake by now. I was excited. "I'll drive and take you all to church tomorrow morning," I told everyone. Finally everyone settled back into bed for a few more hours of sleep.

Sunday morning I got up bright and early ready to take my mother, sisters, and brother to church. Everyone got into the car but Mom. "I'll walk," she said. "It's not too far, and the walk will be good for me."

I could see that she was afraid of my driving, so I didn't beg her to ride.

Now I was ready to haul passengers to and from the NYA job in Waynesville. I had room for five passengers. By the following Monday, which was the start of the two-week work period, I had a full car load of people: four boys and one girl. (There was a female section of the NYA—I don't know what they did. I let the girl out at a building in Waynesville.) I charged each person twenty cents a day for the ride to work and back. This earned me five dollars a week for gas and other expenses to keep the Ford running.

This car never had good breaks or tires as long as I owned it. The brakes were mechanical and needed new linings. The tires all had one or more boots (patches) in them, and the bladders (inner tubes) were covered with patches. I didn't have the money to fix either of these problems.

One afternoon we were on our way home from work on old Highway 19 / 23 near a roadhouse called Little Rock. There weren't many tourists back then, but it happened that one was going to stop at Little Rock just as we came by. He stopped, but I couldn't. My car didn't have any brakes, so I ran directly into the rear end of the tourist's car. No one was hurt, and there was no damage to either car. I apologized to the tourist, we shook hands, and we were on our way again.

I kept the car for about a year and sold it for forty-five dollars. I had plans to go into the Civilian Conservation Corps (CCC). But I also need the money. I sure hated to part with that Ford.

You know what? I never did teach TJ to drive.

Hog Killing Time

One of the most exciting days of late fall or early winter, usually on Thanksgiving or shortly after , the big day that everyone looked forward to every year was called "hog killing time." This would mean that there would be a big feast of fresh cooked meat on the dining table for several days following the hog killing.

You never killed your hogs on a warm day. The weather had to be near the freezing point to consider it the perfect time. As with all other customs and the way that everything had to be done by the people in the mountains of western North Carolina, killing of hogs was a ritual. The hogs had been feeding and getting their winter's supply of nutrition for a full year, and the people were not going to chance the possibility of loosing any of this meat. This would be their supply of meat until the next hog killing.

There were a lot of preparations before the day that the killing took place. The location had to be near a good supply of water. For my family, this was always near the creek where my brother and I took our weekly bath. There was the hanging pole to make. This was for hoisting the hog up to a vertical position with his head hanging down. Next there was the fire place with the dipping vat. This was made from a large metal drum cut in half lengthwise. The fireplace was made from field stone stacked together to hold the dipping vat. It was usually a couple of feet off the ground to allow for the wood that was used for the fire. A table was made from any lumber that was available. It was used for laying the hog on for removing its hair.

We would get up very early on the day of hog killing. There was a still lot of work to do before killing the hog. We built a roaring fire under the dipping vat in which water was placed the day before. With the fire going real good, we would head back to the house for some breakfast. It would be a long day, and we didn't know when we would be in a position to stop long enough to eat again. This was a job that you could not stop and start when you wanted to. Every step of the ritual had you moving according to plans.

Then we would we go to the hog pen with a hammer, a 22 caliber gun, and a long, sharp butcher's knife. Dad would remove some of the boards from the back of the hog pen, shoot the hog between the eyes, pull him out of the pen, and cut his throat with the butchers knife. This seemed gruesome, but the hog had to be bled this way for the meat to be of first quality for our table this winter.

Next the hog was loaded on a one horse sled and taken to the dressing area. After scalding the hog in the boiling water and removing its hair, a one horse singletree was used to prepare for hoisting to a vertical position and the beginning of butchering.

The one doing the cutting had to be very careful not to cut the intestines. The intestines were caught in a large wash tub and sent to the house where the women could remove the fat for rendering for the grease to make lard shorting and lye soap. When everything was removed from the inside of the carcass and it was washed real clean with water that my brother and I carried from the creek, the body was laid on the table that had also been cleaned. Next was the removal of the ribs, back-bones, and tenderloin. The rough blocking (cutting) was done, and the pieces were sent to the house where they would be placed for cooling until the next day.

Now the work for the men was nearly through for the day. They only had the cleaning up of the cleaning area and putting everything back to its storage place. The big part of hog killing was about to begin with the women doing the bigger part of saving the meat. In addition to rendering the lard, there was sausage to make and can, livermush to make from the liver, canning the tenderloin, ribs, and backbones. They would be in the kitchen where it was very warm from the heat of the wood cook stove.

The children also had to quit their playing and help with grinding the sausage with the hand turned grinder that was fastened to the kitchen table. They didn't want to leave the ball game they were having with the hog bladder. They had washed the bladder real clean, inserted a hollow piece of grape vine and filled it with air by blowing through the hollow of the vine wood and tying it with a string to keep the air in. This was a football, a basketball, and a dodge ball until it became dry and shrank.

The work in the kitchen would go on for about three days. The following morning the final trimming of the hams shoulders and middles was done, and then they were placed on a table that was covered with salt in the smokehouse. When all the pieces were in place they were completely covered with salt. The first stage of curing was complete. Later they would be removed from the salt, cleaned, and rubbed with brown sugar and black pepper. Next they were put in cloth sacks and hung from a pole that was the length of the smokehouse and six foot from the floor. In a few weeks they would be ready for eating.

Back to the kitchen. The sausage, liver mush, and cracklings were ready for eating. The best eating was the fried tenderloin along with crackling bread and a glass of cold milk. The liver mush and sausage would be eaten later.

Soon all the work that goes with hog killing was finished. We all were filled with good fresh meat from the hog and were ready to get back to our normal routines. This was setting by a fire in the fireplace, popping corn in the wire corn popper and listening to a story told by one of the grown folks. Hog killing was over until about this time next year.

Grandpa Pressley
Charles Wesley Pressley

Charles Wesley Pressley was my grandpa. To all of his acquaintances and friends he answered to the name of "Charlie." If I asked the younger members of my family about their Great-Great Grandpa "Charlie Pressley," most of them would probably say, "Who was Charlie Pressley?" Therefore, I am writing this brief history of my grandpa's life so that his descendents will know a little about him.

Grandpa Pressley was born in Haywood County in Western North Carolina on October 4, 1879. His father was Devoe Newton Pressley. His mother was Margaret Mehaffey. The two pictures that I have included here are the only ones that I have of Grandpa.

Grandpa Charlie Pressley married Mary Elizabeth Putnam in Clyde, North Carolina, in 1902. They had eight children. They were, in order of their birth:

- William McKinley
  (October 17, 1903 – 1 September 1974)
- Margaret Ellen
  (April 1, 1905 – 15 August 1999)
- D. Alvin
  (February 20, 1907 – 1997)
- Oral Neomia
  (September 24, 1909 – April 28, 1927)
- Charlotte
  (July 10, 1912 – March 8, 1989)
- Doyle Bob
  (September 25, 1914 – July 7, 1975)
- Vernon
  (August 3, 1919 – September 25, 1986)
- Clifford W.
  (July 18, 1920 – January 14, 1982)

In 1999, Margaret Ellen, my mother and the last of Grandpa's eight children, died. That was the end of Grandpa's immediate family. Some of the grandchildren are still living. I am one of them, and I am ninety-one years old.

Grandpa was a descendent of Dutch ancestors. He was not a large man in body, but he was a very hard worker. Life was not easy for Grandpa. He had to work long hours farming on a mountainside to grow food to feed his large family. His children started working to help with chores at a very early age. There was always something they could do to help around the house and in the fields regardless of their age.

In the early part of the spring of 1927, there was a death in the Pressley family. The youngest girl, Oral, 18 years old, died suddenly. She was the fourth child in the family. The cause of her death was uncertain. (Her death certificate says she had pneumonia.)

I was five years old at the time Oral died. I can vividly remember how Grandma and a few neighbors on the mountain prepared Oral for burial. My mom had taken me to the house where her sister was lying in a wooden coffin. There was only one way to bring Oral's body to the Methodist church in the valley for the funeral and burial in the church cemetery. There was a long sled trail around the mountain leading to the house where Grandpa and his family lived. Her coffin was placed on a sled, and it was pulled by a horse to the church. All the family followed along except the twenty-year old brother, Alvin. He would not come into the house while the body of his sister was there, and he did not go to the church for the funeral.

A few days after Oral's burial, Grandpa announced that he was selling his house and belongings and moving to Colorado where the land was flat and he could buy a real farm instead of scratching out a little patch here and there to plant crops to feed his family. Grandpa had been to Colorado several years earlier. In fact, his son Vernon had been born in Colorado in 1919.

Grandpa sent a telegram to his friend in Colorado and asked about buying land. He received a return message saying that there was land for sale. Grandpa bought train tickets the following week, and all of his family, except his daughter Ellen, went by train to Colorado.

Ellen was the second child of the family and was married to Dewey Talmadge Fletcher, and they were living in Gastonia, North Carolina. Talmadge was working in a large cotton mill called the Loray Mill. Ellen and Talmadge were my Mom and Dad. Mom had taken me with her back to Grandpa's house in Haywood County when her sister Oral died.

Our home in Gastonia went back to normal after the funeral and Mom's family's move to Colorado. There were three children in our family in 1927: my brother "TJ" (Talmadge Pressley Fletcher), my baby sister Mary Louise, and me (Charles Clinton

Fletcher), who was the oldest at the age of five. We lived in one of the houses owned by the cotton mill where my dad worked.

Somewhere after midnight one evening, my mom was awakened by smoke in our bedroom. When she got out of bed, she saw that our house was on fire. With her baby girl in her arms and pushing TJ and me in front of her, she had barely got us out into the yard when the whole house exploded into flames. We made it safely to the house of a neighbor who had been awakened by the fire.

Dad was, who was working the night shift in the cotton mill, had seen our house burning while he was on a second story balcony of the factory taking a smoke, not knowing that it was his house. After he received a message that his house was on fire, he came to the neighbor's house where we were. He told us that we would have to go stay with his mother. Dad's mother operated a boarding house on Franklin Avenue in Gastonia.

Our family got into the car that had brought Dad from the cotton mill, and we went to my Grandma Fletcher's house. Grandma was shocked when she saw us with only our night clothes, and we told her about our house burning down. We children went to bed and fell fast asleep, but Mom, Dad, and Grandma spent the rest of the night discussing what we would do next.

Mom and all of Grandpa Pressley's children had always called him "Papa." Mom said, "I'll send Papa a telegram, and he will know what we should do."

Mom and Dad sent a telegram early the next morning, and Grandpa sent a reply that evening. The message read, "Will send train tickets. Come to our house in Greeley, Colorado. Signed: C. Pressley."

"That's what we'll do," Mom said to Dad.

The next few days were spent buying clothes and getting ready for the long train ride out west. By Friday of that week, everything was packed, and we were ready to get on the train. Dad sent Grandpa another telegram that said, "We're on the way. Signed: D.T. Fletcher."

Grandpa Pressley had arranged for someone to meet us at the train station in Greeley, Colorado. He took us to Grandpa's house on the farm.

The following week dad began working for Mr. Green who owned a lot of land near Greeley. Mr. Green provided our family with a house, and we settled into our new home.

When harvest time came that fall, Grandpa had a very good crop of sugar beets that he sold to the sugar refinery. Everything went well for all of us, but Grandpa's family were begging him to move back to North Carolina. Within a few weeks, Grandpa and all his family were on the train heading back to the mountains of western North Carolina. Dad and our family decided to stay in Colorado. Our family was doing well working for Mr. Green.

Then, Mom began to get homesick. She missed her family and began to beg Dad to move back to western North Carolina. So, after the fall crops were harvested, Dad told Mr. Green that we were leaving and returning back east.

Dad bought a "T-Model" Ford touring car that had curtains on the windows on each side. He removed everything from the back seat area. Mom packed it with the keepsakes she wanted and then placed quilts and sheets on top of them. This was to be the bed for my brother, my sister, and me for the next eleven days.

This was in the fall of 1929, and towns and cities were many miles apart. The roads were narrow, and traveling was slow. For a few days we fared very well. Dad had killed about ten ring-neck pheasants the day before we left for the trip, and Mom had packed them in a box. We would stop along the road, Dad would get a fire going, and Mom would prepare a supper of cold biscuits and fried pheasant. We ate pretty well for a few days. Soon, we had to stock up on canned food that we bought when we came to a town. The eating was not very good, but we were able to survive the trip.

Along the way, Dad had to stop and line the bands on the clutch of the car. The clutch wore out really fast. Sometimes he would turn the car around when we came to a steep hill and back up to the top in order to get a few more miles on the clutch. Going in reverse didn't wear out the clutch as much as going forward and changing gears.

Nine days later we were getting close to Canton, North Carolina, our destination. Our money was about gone. Dad sent a telegram to Grandpa asking for money for gas and food for the next two days.

On the evening of the eleventh day, Dad pulled up in front of my Great Aunt Grace's house near Canton in the T-model with all our family in it. The journey back from out west was over. I was seven years old, and I still remember some things about the trip.

This was during the beginning of the Great Depression years of the nineteen-thirties. Jobs were scarce, but luck was with us. Dad got a job in the paper mill in Canton. He would work fourteen hours on the day shift for a week and then ten hours on the second shift for a week. His wages for a two-week pay period came to thirty-five dollars. It was not a very good paying job, but it provided us with more than what people who had no job at all were earning.

Dad rented a house, and we were soon settled down again. This is where I began my schooling. I attended a one-room school close to Aunt Grace's house. It was called the "Austin Chapel School." It had one big room with a coal fired heater in the middle for heat. I attended there one year, and then I went to a new, modern, brick school with seven class rooms, a library, a gymnasium, and an auditorium. The school rooms at the new school were heated by hot water radiators in each room. It was called Beaverdam School. It was one of the modern public schools that were replacing the one-room schools.

Grandpa Pressley didn't move back up on the mountain when he returned from his last trip from Colorado. He had a larger house at the foot of the mountain, but he would go up the mountain to do his farming. His place was only about five miles from where we lived, and every time I had the chance I would go visit his house. I liked to listen to the stories he would tell while I was there.

A Story And A Smile

My youngest uncle, Grandpa's youngest son Clifford, was only seventeen months older than I was, so we seemed like brothers. When we could find at least ten eggs, we would take them to the store in town and sell them at a penny each. Then we would use our money to go to one of the two movie theaters in Canton and spend most of Saturday watching movies, usually westerns. We always watched the shows twice and sometimes more than that. We would act out roping and riding steers and singing songs like the cowboy heroes who we saw in the movies.

On one of my visits to Grandpa's, Clifford and I were helping Grandpa plant his corn up on the mountain near the top. We had finished the corn planting, and Clifford suggested we catch one of the small cows grazing on the mountain and ride it. This sounded great, so we asked grandpa if we could get the galluses off of the overalls that he was using as a scare-crow in his corn patch to use on the calf.

Clifford and I finally hemmed up a calf that probably weighed about two hundred pounds. We tied our make-shift halter on the steer's head, and I was to ride him first. The ride didn't last long for me. I soon found myself lying behind a big log, flat on my back. Clifford decided it was too much trouble to catch another calf for him to ride, so we young cowboys went on home with our grandpa.

On another visit to Grandpa's house, Clifford and I had run out of anything to do but pester Grandpa. Grandpa went outside on the porch and took down what looked like a weed from where it was hanging on the wall. He broke off a couple of small pieces and handed both Clifford and me a piece.

"Chew this up and remember what it tastes like," Grandpa told us.

We both chewed up the root. It left a sweet taste in our mouths.

"What is this?" I asked Grandpa.

"That is ginseng root," Grandpa said. "It grows all over these mountains, and you can sell it for a lot of money. They use it to make medicine."

"Can we go find some?" I asked Grandpa.

"Go on, but be back before dark," Grandpa said. "Go up pretty high on the mountain and look for it around the trees. It looks sort of like a wild onion, and it has that sweet taste."

When Clifford and I came back to Grandpa's house later that evening, our mouths were all puckered and red. We had tasted every weed on the mountain, including wild turnips that would burn your mouth like red hot pepper. Our search for herbs and the dream of getting rich by selling ginseng were over. Grandpa only smiled at us. He had given us something to do instead of hanging around the house all day.

During the Great Depression, it was very hard for ordinary people to feed and care for their families. This was true in Grandpa's case. When President Roosevelt began creating jobs so people could have money to clothe and feed their families, Grandpa was old and could not do hard labor. He got a job as a night watchman where the Work Projects Administration (WPA) were building a new National Guard armory. On one of my visits, Grandpa let me spend the night with him while he was night watchman at the armory. He would go all over the site every hour and turn a key in clocks at different stations. It was a big treat for me to feel like I was helping him.

Grandpa was a humble, easy-going man who had never done any harm to any of his fellowmen. He was very strict with his five boys. He never used alcohol in any form. He did, nevertheless, tolerate Grandma's having what she called her "medicine," which was two big spoons-full of moonshine whiskey mixed with sugar and water before each meal.

Grandpa's chewed apple-flavored chewing tobacco. You would always see him wearing his denim overalls with his plug of apple tobacco in the pocket on the chest of the overalls.

I liked being with my grandpa, but as I grew older I saw less of him. I tried to visit him when it was convenient. I saw him even less often after Grandma died. He was seldom at home after she died. When weather permitted, he would spend his days sitting on a bench with some of his older friends in a park beside the main street in town. He had a lot in common with his friends. They all chewed tobacco and talked about the latest happenings and swapped knives every once in a while.

Whenever possible, I would find Grandpa and visit with him. However, as I grew older, I had less time to visit. I joined the Civilian Conservation Corps (CCC), I was in the US Army during WWII, and I got married and started raising a family of my own, so I very seldom saw Grandpa.

In 1953 I moved to Tennessee where I had found new employment, and I never saw Grandpa again. He died in 1953, the same year that I moved away. He was 73 years old. He was hit by a car while crossing the street in town, and he died at his daughter's home several months later.

Grandpa Pressley was a hard worker, he raised a large family, and he was never afraid to venture out and seek a better life for his family. Charles Wesley Pressley was a great man, and I am proud to have been named after him.

www.ingramcontent.com/pod-product-compliance
Lightning Source LLC
LaVergne TN
LVHW021716060526
838200LV00050B/2690